THE GHOST OF THE PANNELL WITCH

A SHORT STORY COLLECTION

MELISSA MANNERS

MELISSA MANNERS PUBLISHING

For the residents of Kippax, who are the reason these legends survive

INTRODUCTION

This is a collection of short stories based on Mary Pannell, the subject of my debut novel, *The Pannell Witch*.

Please note that one of these stories, *Descendant*, follows the same plot as *The Pannell Witch*, and so this one contains spoilers!

Mary Pannell's stories have been orally passed down for over four hundred years, resulting in multiple versions of her tale.

Unfortunately, many of the historical records concerning Mary Pannell have been lost over the years, including her court records. The parish records of Kippax are available online, and one can use this to confirm that she existed. She was born in 1538, with her name recorded as Marye Tailer. In 1559, at twenty-one, she married John Pannell, one year older than her, and together they had four children, two of whom survived to adulthood. Namely Elizabeth, born in 1569 and Agnes, in 1575.

Mary was reportedly employed as a servant or nursery maid at Ledston Hall, an ancient monastery that served as the Witham family's residence. The parish records confirm that the couple who lived there were William Witham, born in 1546, and Eleanor Witham (née Neale), born in 1552. They had eleven children between the years of 1573-1590, the most well-known of whom grew up to be known as Dame Mary Bolles, born in 1579. King Charles I granted her the title of Baronet, and as the only woman to have ever received this honour, she signed her name Baronetesse. The other well-known Witham child, William Witham, was born in 1588 and died at five years old in 1593.

Many people claim the authorities arrested Mary Pannell for witchcraft in 1593, but there are varied reasons given for this. One story is that Mary was having an affair with William Witham, and then later murdered him. His wife Eleanor may have falsely accused her of witchcraft as an act of revenge. Because of the sheer influence of the Witham family, it is possible that this led to Mary's conviction for witchcraft.

Others say she had a reputation as a wise woman who provided medicines and herbal remedies to the residents. Some versions of her story involve one of her medicines going terribly wrong. In particular, it is said that she provided medicine to the young William Witham who had a nasty cough, but that instead of being spread on his chest, he ingested it, for whatever reason, which caused his death. Mary may have been blamed for his death, and thus arrested in 1593.

Mary's execution did not take place until ten years later, in 1603. There are few convincing reasons for such a long period between her alleged arrest and execution. Even so, one is presented in *The Pannell Witch*.

The stories don't seem to agree on where exactly Mary was executed. It seems likely that she would have been hanged at York, where her trial would have taken place, and then her body brought back to Kippax, perhaps on the hill that bears her name, to be burned. However, there is a lack of evidence and she may, in fact, have been executed on that hill.

Legend has it that Mary's ghost haunts the local area to this day. Some say that if you see her ghost, then one of your relatives will soon die. Others think it more likely that her ghost is a friendly sort of presence, and would never hurt the residents of the town that she once helped with her own herbal remedies.

Each story presents a unique perspective on Mary's life and death, drawing from different legends.

DISTURBANCE

A police officer has one last chance to investigate the strange happenings up on the Mary Pannell.

With the help of the locals, can find the cause of the sightings before it's too late?

1

MEETING

'DS Payne,' her boss sighed. 'If you can't manage the disturbance yourself, how can you expect a promotion?' He was wearing a smart enough suit, but it was tatty, old. His shirt was creased. To her, he had always seemed like he was tired, ready to go home. But he had been in the job for *years* and showed no intention of leaving.

Amanda Payne bit her lip. 'Sir, please. No one will talk seriously to me about this case. Talk of strange things is everywhere. I've been living here for months now and I *still* don't understand this town.'

He frowned. 'Kippax is a beautiful place, full of history. If you can't handle it, I think you'll find the blame lies solely on yourself.'

'No, sir—I didn't mean—' She could tell she had offended him, and though that hadn't been her intention, it was no secret that she didn't like it here.

'Would you rather I take you off the case? I can reassign it. Perhaps move you to something more simple. I can put you back on traffic.' He reached out to flick through a stack of papers on his desk. 'Ah, here we go. I'll just need you to sign this—'

'No,' she interrupted, her voice firm. 'I can do this. I know I can.' She thought of her children, living down in London with their father. She *needed* this promotion to be transferred back to the city, finally. 'I just need time to find them, to uncover the individual behind these complaints.'

He peeked at her over his glasses. 'Hmm. I wish I could help you. But this has dragged on for too long. First thing tomorrow, I'm reassigning this case. Missing persons can have it.'

Her heart sank. After all her effort in the recent months? It wasn't fair. 'But sir, if I could just—'

'That's enough, DS Payne,' he sighed. 'I trust you can see yourself out.' He gestured to his office door.

What else could she do? She plastered on the best smile she could and stood to leave. 'Yes, sir.'

2

WHITE HORSE

Amanda knew she could drive to London that evening. But she couldn't handle the traffic at this time of night and didn't want to spend hours waiting in queues on the motorway. Especially when her children might be in bed by the time she arrived. There was no guarantee her ex-husband would let her in, anyway. No, it wasn't a good idea.

Instead, she drove along Pannell Hill, trying to look for anyone hiding in the shadows between the trees. In the absence of other cars, she slowed down and squinted, attempting to see anything amidst the dark tree trunks and interlocking branches. There were no signs of movement. Not even a bird or a fox.

The toot of a car's horn made her jump, and she realised she had come to a stop. She shot the driver behind her a guilty look in her rearview mirror and held up a hand in apology. She sped up and, almost without thinking, drove towards Ledston. Eventually, the car behind turned off, leaving her alone on the road. There was no sign of anything unusual happening. Every time she searched the hill area, there was nothing to discover. There would be reports of disturbances and sightings the very next day. Some would say they heard screams.

Amanda groaned and hit her steering wheel in frustration. She *had* to solve this case. But it was too late. She hadn't managed to get the locals on side during her time here. There was only one thing for it. She turned into the car park upon seeing the old pub, The White Horse. She threw her jacket onto the backseat, and instead put on the denim jacket she kept in there. Her hair, forever pinned up into a high bun, was released, loose waves falling down her shoulders. Amanda was never one to wear much makeup, but on this night, she put on a thin layer of red lipstick, smacking her lips and surveying her reflection in the small mirror. That would do. At least she looked less like a police officer now, and more like an average person.

The White Horse was an old Tudor pub, with exposed brick walls and original wooden beams across the ceiling. Outside, deep green ivy covered one side of the pub, and on the inside, there were plants everywhere that gave it a cosy feel. She'd driven past it plenty of times, but never actually been inside. When she entered, there were several tables where people were sitting down, eating. There was a cosier area on the other side of the pub with a lit fireplace, smaller tables, and a line of stools at the bar. She exhaled softly. Hopefully, she wouldn't attract as much attention here. Some people over here appeared to be by themselves. Next to her, an older couple conversed quietly, while a man read a newspaper nearby.

'What can I get you, officer?' The young man behind the bar asked brightly, in a strong Yorkshire accent.

She scoffed, taking a seat at the bar. 'How did you—have we met?'

He grinned. 'I've seen you around. I'm Tom,' he said with a nod.

'Amanda,' she replied. 'Just a half of lager for me, please. With a splash of lime.'

He kept his eyes on her while he pulled the tap down.

'I'm off duty,' she blurted out.

Tom raised an eyebrow. 'No judgement from me, ma'am,' he promised. He poured a small amount of lime cordial into the glass and held out the card reader for her to pay.

'She's driving, so she'll likely only take the one,' a woman said, walking in behind her.

Amanda span around in her seat, already cross at the attitude of these people. 'Excuse me?'

The woman walking towards her was slightly older than her, perhaps thirty years old, and wore a long, flowing purple skirt and loose blouse. She was absolutely covered in jewellery—gold, silver, colourful. Her outfit appeared to have zero cohesion, and she wore thick-rimmed glasses, with tight ringlets framing her dark-skinned face. She gave her a warm smile. 'Not to worry, my dear,' she reassured her. 'I popped in just after you. Saw you fixing your makeup before you came in.'

Amanda's cheeks heated. But she supposed it wasn't a crime for this woman to have seen her coming into the pub. 'And your name is...?'

She smirked. 'I'm Robin. Lovely to meet you, Amanda.' She took a seat at the bar next to her and gave Tom a nod. He poured her a glass of white wine without needing to ask.

Amanda was unable to avert her gaze. At Robin's wrist, her sleeve rode up slightly, to reveal the edge of some kind of tattoo, though she couldn't make out the shape. At her neck she wore a thick silver chain with some kind of symbol on the pendant, and in her ears she wore similar, but not identical, gold dangling stars.

'They're part of a set,' Robin said.

Amanda's eyes widened. 'I—I didn't mean to stare,' she said quickly.

Robin shrugged, taking a sip of her wine. 'It's quite alright. I'm used to it. My sister has the other earrings.'

She could feel Tom's eyes on them both, watching them, but for a moment she didn't care. She had an overwhelming urge to know everything about Robin. 'Does she live far away?'

'You could say that,' Robin said, her voice going slightly higher.

Amanda was always very literal. She had little tolerance for metaphors and avoiding the truth. It was a factor in her being a great police officer. Still, she tried not to sound too annoyed when she asked, 'is she abroad?'

'She's dead,' Robin said simply.

'Fuck,' Amanda muttered under her breath. 'I didn't realise—I'm sorry.'

'You didn't know.'

They each sipped their drinks and said nothing for a while.

'So, tell me,' Robin said eventually, the tips of her eyelashes glinting in the firelight. 'What made you decide to grace us with your presence tonight, after months of living here?'

Amanda scoffed. 'You're talking like I haven't even been here.'

'Have you?' Robin asked, the edge of her lip curling up into a smile.

'Well, I—I visit London sometimes, on the weekends,' she admitted.

'You mean every weekend,' Robin corrected her.

Amanda sighed, agitated now. What business was it of hers where she spent her weekends? 'Fine, I go down there a lot. But I have to—my children live there.'

'Ah,' Robin said.

'Their father is—' She prepared herself to explain, not the whole story, but the abridged version she had practised well enough to tell to strangers who demanded some sort of explanation.

'Don't,' she said, raising her hand. 'Don't feel like you have to explain if you don't want to.'

Amanda breathed a sigh of relief. 'Okay,' she murmured.

'But I am interested in why you're here tonight,' Robin said.

'Oh, right. Of course.' Amanda gulped down more of her drink and noticed the other people around them had quietened their own conversations. Not subtle at all. 'I, um —I think my investigation is over. I haven't been able to solve it. You know—the situation on Pannell Hill.'

Robin smirked. 'I know you've spoken to plenty of witnesses. You have all the information you could possibly need.'

The man glanced up from his newspaper. 'I spoke to her weeks ago. Told her about that time I saw Mary's ghost myself! But would she listen? Hm!'

Amanda sighed. Not this again. 'Well, with all due respect, sir—'

'Nor me,' the older lady interrupted, the one sitting next to Robin at the bar. 'I told her about that time I heard Mary, clear as day. I was walking along, and she ran through the trees, obviously not wanting to be seen. Straight away I called back, saying I wasn't there to do her any harm, but who knows if she was listening?'

'Please, I just think that, until we know who's *really* causing all this, that we should just—'

'What? You don't believe eye witnesses? Is that it?'

'Leave her alone,' Tom implored him. 'She's new. She has no knowledge of the history.'

Amanda was fed up with everyone acting so bloody patronising. She slammed her beer on the bar and tried to keep her voice steady. "I'm well aware of the Mary Pannell legend," she said, emphasizing 'legend' to indicate the scarcity of evidence surrounding her alleged witchcraft accusation. 'There have been incidents of theft, public antagonism, and a few weeks ago there was an assault on a young man.'

Robin raised an eyebrow. 'A young man who tried to force himself on his girlfriend that very night.'

Amanda held up a hand. 'No one has been able to prove that.'

'Well, I think that's evidence that it's Mary up there. The ghost's only aggressive act was in defense of a woman.'

'Supposedly,' Amanda said.

Robin rolled her eyes. 'Well then, Amanda. I mean, Officer—?' Her tone went high-pitched, questioning.

'Payne. I'm DS Payne.'

'Officer Payne,' she grinned. 'What do you think of heading up there tonight? See if we can separate fact from fiction?'

Amanda glanced towards her almost empty glass. 'Um, I was going to go in the morning,' she began.

'Nonsense,' declared Robin. 'Mary's much more likely to reveal herself at night.'

Amanda couldn't help but sigh.

'Enough of that scepticism,' Robin said. 'You won't need it after you see her in person.'

She had to admit that whoever it was; they *were* more likely to reveal themselves at night. 'Fine,' she breathed. 'We'll go tonight.'

Tom cleared his throat. 'Want some company?' He asked. 'If you're willing to wait a couple of hours, I'll close up here and come along.'

'Aye, as will I,' the man said from behind them. He folded up his newspaper and cleared his throat. 'You'll need all the help you can get, from the sounds of it.'

Amanda leaned back in her chair, crossing her arms. 'Really, I don't need help. I have plenty of experience.'

Robin smirked. 'Do you?'

'Yes.' Amanda's cheeks heated once more. The heat from the fireplace felt overwhelming all of a sudden. 'I have years of experience in the force. I joined up right before I got married.'

'You're married?' Robin's face fell ever so slightly.

'No,' she said. 'I mean, not anymore.' The pub seemed to have gone quiet all of a sudden, with everyone listening eagerly to them. 'I'm divorced,' she clarified.

'Ah,' Robin replied, a smile gracing her face. 'Sorry to hear that.' She didn't look the slightest bit sorry.

'Anyway,' the woman next to them said. 'We're coming too.' She gestured to her husband.

'I'll just drive up—' Amanda began.

The woman choked out a laugh.

'What?' Amanda asked, indignant.

'No, love,' she breathed. 'You won't be driving up there. There's nowhere to park, and if you're planning on driving right up to the woods, you'll spook her. You want to meet her, don't you?'

The way these people spoke, it was like Mary was a living, breathing resident of the town. It was exhausting, arguing with it the whole time. Her energy was depleted and her boss suggested she wouldn't be on the case for much longer, anyway. Perhaps it was easier to just go along with it. 'Yes,' she said finally. 'Yes, I want to meet Mary.'

Robin shot her a satisfied grin. 'Good. We'll all walk up in a couple of hours, just after closing.' She raised her voice. 'Anyone who wants to walk up the Mary Pannell, come and walk with us.'

'Hell, no,' a middle-aged man's voice rang out from nearby tables.

'You scared?' Robin smirked.

'Too right I am!' He said, taking a gulp of his pint.

'Same here,' another man chimed in. 'We've all heard the stories. Whether or not it's true, I'm not risking it.'

'Cowards,' a woman shot at them. 'I'm not afraid of Mary. Whatever's happening up there, I know Mary's not the one hurting people. She's one of us, born and raised.'

Hushed voices murmured in agreement, and gradually a low chatter spread once more around the pretty pub.

'Another?' Tom asked.

'Yes, please,' Robin answered for her. 'On me.'

'You don't have to—'

'I'd like to,' she said. 'As a thank you for letting us show you the truth of the legend of Mary Pannell.'

3

PANNELL HILL

A fter a couple of hours of talking, Amanda decided Robin wasn't that bad. Prior to that night, she hadn't actually spoken to her, but they'd seen each other around. Robin earned a living from her crystal business, and she was also well-known in the area for her tarot readings.

'Would you let me read your tarot?' Robin asked her, as she drained her second glass of wine.

Amanda sighed. 'Um...' she trailed off. She had no desire to offend her. In fact, Robin seemed perfectly lovely. But that didn't mean Amanda suddenly believed in the supernatural.

'It's okay,' she said, her voice silky smooth, even as it slurred ever so slightly. 'I know you don't believe in it.'

She shrugged. 'I just don't see the point.'

'Is that why you never called me in for questioning?' Robin said.

Amanda was caught off-guard. She hadn't considered that Robin would have noticed this. 'How did you—?'

'I know I was on the witness lists,' she said. 'Most of the

others were called in for interviews with you. That or they spoke to you when you did the door-to-doors.'

Amanda drained the last of her half of lager and lime. 'Look,' she said, unable to wipe the guilty look off her face. 'It's not that I didn't want to hear from you. It's just—'

'You knew I'd tell you it's the ghost of Mary Pannell who's behind all this,' she interrupted.

Amanda hesitated. 'Well, yes.'

'And you've already decided that, no matter the evidence to the contrary, ghosts don't exist?' Robin raised an eyebrow.

'I did *not* say that,' Amanda said, though she was struggling to keep her thoughts straight. The fire had gone out, leaving Tom to clear away the glasses in the cold. People inside the pub were filtering out. 'I base my decisions on the evidence. And the evidence shows that the people in this area *are inclined* to believe in the legend of Mary Pannell. I believe people *think* they've seen her.'

Robin rolled her eyes. 'I suppose that's progress.'

'How about this? I promise to believe you *if* I find evidence to support your theory?'

She choked out a laugh. 'That hardly means anything. Only that you're not going to be so arrogant as to refuse the truth when it's in front of you.'

Amanda shrugged. 'There are plenty of people who would do just that in this situation.'

'Mm, I suppose that's true,' she conceded. 'Fine. I accept your terms, *Amanda*.' She held out a hand for Amanda to shake.

Amanda's whole body shivered at the sound of her first name on the tip of Robin's tongue. She shook her hand, and then jumped when Tom turned on the lights, and she was confronted with Robin's face, actually visible in the artificial light of the pub. She was as beautiful in this setting as she was in the firelight.

She pulled back her hand quickly and glanced over to Tom.

'Anyone who's walking up the Mary Pannell, follow DS Payne,' he called.

There was a quiet buzz of excitement as they left the pub, with Tom locking up afterward.

Amanda and Robin led the way, walking close together.

Amanda took out her phone and shot off a quick text. 'It's just my ex-husband,' she said, and then chastised herself for not being clear. It was almost midnight, and she had just told this woman she was texting her ex. 'I'm checking on the kids,' she clarified, as she put her phone back in her back pocket.

Robin nodded, smiling gently. 'You're a good mother.'

Amanda scoffed. 'Nobody has *ever* described me that way. I'm not even a good *person*.' She immediately regretted her words when she saw, lit only by the dim streetlights, the way her face fell.

'Don't talk about yourself like that,' Robin murmured, her voice quiet but firm.

Amanda avoided meeting Robin's eye, keeping her gaze on the ground. The grass was wet, and dampened the bottom of her trousers, but she didn't care. Right now, she was just worried she'd pissed off Robin. Worried she'd been too honest. 'I only meant—I just—I've made some poor decisions. I've hurt people,' she said eventually. 'Sorry.'

'It's okay,' Robin said. 'It's just that you sound just like my sister.'

'Were you close?' Amanda asked, relieved that the conversation had moved away from her.

'Closer than anyone realised,' she murmured. 'We were twins.'

Amanda didn't miss the use of the past tense. *Fuck*. Glancing back, she saw Tom engrossed in conversation with another man a short distance away. They wouldn't be overheard. 'You lost her recently?' Amanda asked, before adding quickly, 'you don't have to tell me.'

Robin shrugged. 'I enjoy talking about her. Makes me feel like she's still with me, you know?' Her smile was tinged with sadness.

'I understand,' Amanda replied. She was out of breath now, making her way up the slight incline, ankles now drenched from the wet grass.

'It was a few months ago.' Robin hesitated for a few seconds before adding, 'I wish she'd felt able to come to me first.'

'Sometimes it's not that easy,' Amanda whispered, her voice almost lost in the whistle of the wind.

Robin tucked her hair back, tying it into a low ponytail so that the wind would stop blowing it in her face. 'Sounds like you're speaking from experience.'

Amanda's eyes locked with Robin's, pausing before revealing too much.

'Here we are.' Tom's voice brought her back to the moment.

Once they crossed the road, Amanda noticed the woods rumored to be haunted by Mary Pannell's ghost.

'So what is it you're actually investigating?' Robin asked Amanda.

'There have always been suspicious reports around here,' she whispered, gesturing to the woods. 'It started off with reports of sightings—we figured it was kids sneaking up there at night, you know?'

The others crowded around, eager to hear what she had to say.

'My department has always dismissed it as superstition. People believe there's a ghost, so they believe they see the ghost.'

'Until now?' Robin asked.

'Until about six months ago. It started off with increased reports of littering. Then people were ringing us, saying they heard screaming in the night.'

'Mary was screaming?' The man from the pub asked, looking at his wife.

'*Someone* was screaming,' Amanda corrected. 'Supposedly.'

Robin smirked, looking over to the woods. The leaves moved about in the wind, in such a way that if someone were flitting between the trees, they wouldn't be noticed.

'Anyway, we think there might be a homeless person living up there,' she said. 'But I haven't found them any time I've gone up to look around.' She didn't mention that a patient had gone missing from the local hospital a few months prior. For all she knew, it was unrelated.

Robin frowned, as if the idea that the disturbance was caused by anyone but Mary's ghost was ridiculous. 'Well, I suppose we'll find out soon enough.'

'We'll go up together, but in small groups,' Amanda murmured. 'Twos or threes, at the least. I want to ensure nobody is left on their own.' It was all adults, and it wasn't like this was a crime scene. If they wanted to come up, she had no reason to keep them out. 'If you're in danger, you shout out and I'll come running. Understood?' Her tone was stern, and she didn't ask if anyone had any questions. She just took Robin, grabbing her wrist, and led her up to the dark expanse of trees.

4

THE PANNELL WITCH

I t was somehow both quieter and louder up here. Away from the low thrum of voices coming from behind them, it seemed quieter. The wind drowned out all other sounds, and Amanda was certain they were being followed because of the cracking branches. At the sound of something falling, her head snapped around.

Robin put a hand on her shoulder. 'It's okay,' she whispered. 'It was just an animal. A fox or something.'

'Did you see a fox anywhere?' Amanda hissed.

'Well, no.'

Amanda brushed her hand off her shoulder. She didn't need someone to hold her hand while walking in the woods. She was a police officer, for goodness' sake. 'I can handle myself,' she murmured.

'Of course.'

She knelt down and picked up a browned apple core. Someone had clearly bitten into it. Signs of life. She reached into her pocket for an evidence bag and slipped it inside.

'You really think that's evidence of anything?' Robin asked under her breath.

'Discovering someone would suggest they've been staying here.'

In the dark, Amanda barely saw Robin roll her eyes under the moonlit trees. She had a torch, but didn't want to startle anyone who might be hiding here.

'Shh, stay here,' Amanda said, holding a finger to her lips. As she walked through trees, she kept an eye on the ground until Robin took her hand.

'Be careful,' she whispered.

Amanda kept her eyes locked on hers, but didn't stop walking. She kept going, through the leaf-covered ground that seemed to go downhill ever so slightly until—'ah!' She let out a yelp as she fell down the edge of a hill. It was steeper than it looked and she rolled down, only coming to a stop when she got right to the bottom.

'Shit, shit, shit,' she murmured, when a wave of pain washed over her. Stupid.

'Are you okay?' Robin called. 'Stay there, I'll come down.'

'No!' Amanda shouted back. 'I'm—I'm fine. Don't come down this way, you'll hurt yourself.' She knew how she sounded, but there was no point in Robin being injured, too.

'Can you walk?' Robin's voice was softer this time, and it made Amanda *ache*.

She pushed herself up to a kneeling position, but when she tried to step onto her ankle, she screamed in pain. 'No,' she managed.

'Wait for me,' she called. 'I'll be quick.'

Amanda collapsed back into a seated position, leaning against a jagged rock. She heard footsteps and voices in the distance, which was no surprise given the large group in the woods. It was the voice on the wind that sent a shiver down her spine. 'Hello?' She called.

There was no response. The wind whistled past her ears,

bringing a shiver out of her. The voices in the distance were gone. There was no sign of Robin.

'If you've been staying here, I can help you,' she tried. 'Elizabeth?'

The wind seemed to go silent at that. At the name of the patient who had gone missing from the psychiatric ward at the local hospital.

'Elizabeth, it's not safe for you here,' Amanda said, kneeling up once more, and glancing around to see if the patient was there. She had the distinct feeling she was being watched. If they belonged to their group, they would have come up to her and checked on her. 'But I can keep you safe if you come with me.'

A blast of icy wind hit her in the face, and she was pushed back onto her knees.

Amanda let out a yelp. She snapped her head around in one direction, and then the other. No one seemed to be there. 'Hello?'

When there was no reply, she tried again. 'Elizabeth?'

'She's safe with me.' The voice was almost a whisper, travelling along the lines of the wind, and Amanda was almost certain she had imagined it.

A chill ran right down Amanda's spine. 'Mary?' She asked, this time in just a whisper. But she still couldn't see her. Surely it was Elizabeth, the patient, but what if she was pretending to be Mary? 'I'm not going to hurt you, Mary,' she called.

There was a long pause, and eventually, Amanda caught sight of a row of rough green leaves. She was sure they hadn't been there before.

'Wrap them around your ankle,' the voice told her, louder this time, as if its owner had come closer.

Amanda whipped her head around. However, she saw

no one there. She tore off one of the leaves and inspected it. In the darkness, she could just about make out the lines running along it. 'Is this... cabbage?' She asked.

The absence of a response elicited a sigh from Amanda. She tore off a couple more of the leaves and wrapped them around her ankle. 'Fine,' she muttered. 'I'll do it. Like this?' She tried to stand, but the shapeless gust of wind knocked her back again.

'Wait.'

She scoffed. 'Okay, I'm waiting. But you have to show yourself at some point.'

There was silence again.

'You know they had you on suicide watch?' Amanda asks quietly. 'Your family thinks they've lost you already.'

The coldest wind yet blew past her ears and the words hit her before she knew what was happening. 'I kept her safe.'

'Wait, what? You mean—?' Amanda sputtered over her words. She knew—she was certain—that this wasn't the ghost of Mary speaking. It had to be Elizabeth, somehow. 'Did you try to hurt yourself? Is that why you're out here?'

Robin emerged in the gap as footsteps echoed through the trees. 'Manda,' she cooed, her voice soft. 'Can you still not walk?' A look of concern covered her face.

Amanda knew she shouldn't melt like she was, but no one ever called her that. She struggled to stand, but the cabbage leaves had relieved enough pain for her to do so. She frowned. 'How did she—?'

Robin took the cabbage and inspected it. 'Ah,' she said, nodding. 'Mary helped you.'

She shook her head. 'No, the *other* woman did. She won't show herself, but she pointed out the cabbage leaves, explained how to use them on my ankle.'

Robin smirked. 'No, love. It was Mary.'

'Actually, it was Elizabeth.' She scolded herself for saying it as soon as she did. The name of the woman from the hospital was confidential. She wasn't supposed to mention it to anyone.

'Elizabeth?' Robin asked, her body going stock still.

'Shit, sorry. Forget I said that.' Amanda stood up, holding onto Robin for support.

'No, wait. The person you think is hiding out here, she's called Elizabeth?' Robin held her gently, one arm sliding around her waist.

Amanda shrugged, doing her best not to shiver at Robin's touch. 'Well, yeah. She's missing, and the timing matches up. I'm surprised at how long she's managed to stay hidden...'

'Manda—you said you knew the legend, right?' Robin's voice was soft.

'What? Of course. They say Mary was accused of witch-craft, and then executed,' Amanda said simply. She did her research, as much as she had to, if for no other reason than to understand the locals.

Robin's lips curled up into a smile, and she rubbed circles onto her waist. 'Manda, she had a girlfriend. A romantic partner.' She paused before clarifying, 'Elizabeth.'

Amanda shook her head. 'You can't actually think—'

'Actually, I can. I think Mary's been keeping this woman safe, because she reminds her of her partner.'

'I never thought people back then *were*—'

'Gay? Lesbian?' Robin asked plainly. 'Manda, queer people have always existed. But I think, in Mary's time, people turned a blind eye to women in relationships with other women. Until it suited them better not to.' Her grip on Amanda seemed to loosen slightly.

Amanda frowned, limping as she walked. It was more difficult when Robin wasn't holding onto her so tightly, but she refused to ask for help. 'What do you mean?'

Robin sighed, not seeming to notice Amanda's struggle with walking. 'All I'm saying is that those accused of witchcraft were targeted. There must have been some reason her friends and neighbours turned against her. And it's no secret that a lot of accused witches lived their lives away from men.'

'How could you possibly know that?' Amanda asked. Because she couldn't, could she?

'I see certain things,' Robin mused, her tongue running gently over her top lip. 'I rarely get much, but sometimes there are pictures. Snapshots, if you like.'

Amanda didn't want to be rude. For all she knew, Robin could see many things about Mary, about how she lived her life. 'I prefer to base my opinions on evidence,' she said, trying to keep her tone steady. She hoped Robin wouldn't be offended.

Robin rolled her eyes and stopped, pulling away and staring back at Amanda. 'I saw you coming, you know.'

Amanda scoffed, crossing her arms as she looked back at Robin, meeting her gaze head-on. 'What are you talking about?'

'Exactly that,' she said, gesturing to her. 'I saw an image of you, right here. Walking through these woods with me.'

She couldn't quite believe what this woman was saying. 'If that's actually true, why didn't you just say that? In the pub, you acted like you didn't know me.'

'To be fair, you wouldn't have believed me. Besides, I didn't know you. I didn't know your name.'

'Why should I believe you?'

Robin hummed in thought, and her eyes seemed to pore

into her mind. 'Your children are lovely,' she murmured. 'You think about them a lot.'

Amanda made a frustrated sort of sound. What sort of stalker was this woman?

Her voice was gentle, like she didn't want to spook her. 'I don't know their names, but I know you have a boy and a girl. The girl is taller, but she looks younger. She likes to wear her hair down and hates anyone brushing it and tying it back. Your boy is quieter. He can be shy and withdrawn sometimes. Except when he fights with his sister. He always starts it. Like at that visit to the—park? No, the zoo.' Robin looked wistful as she described them, like she was seeing images in her mind even as she spoke.

'That's really creepy.'

'Mm, so I've been told,' Robin said.

This woman was clearly strange. She knew things she shouldn't. There was no way Amanda trusted her. She made a mental note to run a background check as soon as she was back at work. It could be that she was into something dangerous, that there was some specific reason that she had looked into Amanda's life. She shivered at the thought that she had even done some research on her children. But for now, at least, she knew they were safe with her father, and Amanda could keep an eye on Robin.

For now, Amanda thought it would be best simply to go along with it. If she could get Robin to let her guard down, she might reveal something about herself. About who she really was. How she really came by her information. So she took a deep breath and asked, 'you really think Mary was executed because of her sexuality?' She walked on, trying to keep her weight on her strong leg. Her limp wasn't likely to go away anytime soon.

Robin shrugged, one arm easily sliding back around

Amanda's waist to support her. 'I don't think it was that simple. But I think she was a wise woman. Known in her community for her abilities.' There was a glint in her eyes, and Amanda imagined Robin could relate to Mary. Perhaps that was why she saw snapshots of her life. 'She was trusted, for a long time, to cure the ailments of her friends and neighbours, but ultimately, she lived on the edges of society.'

Amanda furrowed her brow, refusing to acknowledge how grateful she was to Robin for essentially holding her up as she walked. She really hoped this woman wasn't danger-ous, because she was in no state to fight back tonight. She hoped the rest of their group were still within earshot, just in case she had to shout for help. 'What do you mean?'

'She lived with her two daughters and a female romantic partner. I don't think she put all that much effort into hiding it, because for much of her life, nobody paid her much attention. They lived on the outside of town, and that was the life they chose. The life that made them happy. For a time.'

'Until?' It was getting darker by the minute, and it was near impossible to see where she was walking, but somehow Robin managed to direct them along a fairly flat path.

'Until people turned against her. People can be very hypocritical,' she sighed. 'Even though she may have been trusted by and large, people have always feared what they don't understand. And so, when things in the community started to go wrong, she was blamed.'

'Blamed for what?' Amanda asked quietly.

'Everything. Failed harvests, animals falling sick, even miscarriages. From what I've seen, all sorts of crimes were piled on her, and she crumbled under the sheer weight of the accusations. She didn't stand a chance.'

Amanda didn't say anything to that. Whether or not Robin really saw these things, it was doubtless true that many women did face exactly this fate. They continued to walk the impossible-to-see path, dried leaves crunching under their feet.

'I just don't know what she's trying to keep her safe from.' Robin muttered, screwing up her face, as if trying to work out what the reason could be.

'I, um—I think I might know the answer to that,' Amanda admitted. Although there was no way this story could be true, she also wanted to solve this case, once and for all. She glanced around them, trying to catch a glimpse of Elizabeth.

'Yeah?' Robin asked.

'I think she came here in an attempt to end her life.'

Robin went still once more, her grip on Amanda tightening.

'I tried to tell her I could help her, but I'm the last person who can promise that,' she sighed. She clutched Robin tightly, not wanting to let go. Tears welled up in her eyes, and she didn't want to continue this conversation anymore.

'Why's that?' Robin asked quietly.

Amanda bit her lip. 'I, um—I can understand the feeling, that's all.'

Even in the dark, Robin met her gaze. She wiped Amanda's cheeks dry from tears she hadn't even realised were falling. 'It's something you've tried to do,' she said simply. Her face fell in horror as she stared off into space. Like she could see it. Though, of course, that was ridiculous.

Amanda nodded. She didn't have the words to explain, but she found herself explaining it, anyway. She wanted to get it off her chest.

'What happened?'

'My, um—my children found me.' Amanda's cheeks burned with shame. She wasn't even sure why she was revealing this ugly part of herself. The part she kept hidden down deep. She choked out a sob and added, 'they weren't supposed to come back. My husband—at the time— brought them home early, and—' She couldn't go on any more as the sobs overtook her body. 'I'm sorry. I'm so sorry. I don't know why I'm telling you this.' This suspicious woman was certainly not the right person to open up to, but for some reason, she trusted her. With this, anyway.

Robin turned to face her and put her index finger under her chin, tilting her face up slightly. 'I'm sorry that happened to you,' she murmured. 'But I'm so glad you're here right now.'

Amanda wrapped her arms tightly around Robin. She didn't know what to say to that. 'I shouldn't have—I don't know why I just—you didn't need me to trauma dump—' She sobbed between each breath, hating how utterly pathetic she sounded. Especially in front of Robin. This was *humiliating*.

'It's how my sister died,' Robin admitted, after a moment of silence.

'Fuck,' Amanda muttered, eyes widening. She pulled back and looked Robin in the eye. Her eyes were bright even in the deep woods, the moonlight hitting her face just right. She was taller than Robin, and the way she looked down at her made her feel like she was the only person who mattered. She felt like she *mattered*. Without thinking, she rose onto her tiptoes, bringing her lips up.

'Hello?' The croaky voice of a young woman broke Amanda out of her headspace.

'What?' she snapped, head turning around until she was face-to-face with her.

She matched the headshot Amanda had found, but only just. Her hair was ratty, with small twigs and leaves tangled up in it. She wore the hospital gown as expected, but it was ripped almost to shreds.

Around them, numerous footsteps sounded. It seemed that as soon as Elizabeth had revealed herself, the rest of their group had managed to find them at the bottom of the hill. Where they had been hiding until that point, Amanda had no idea. But right now, they were all standing there, watching the scene unfold. Staring at Elizabeth, wearing only rags.

'Elizabeth?' Amanda sputtered. She tore off her denim jacket quickly and offered it to the woman, who flinched.

'I won't hurt you,' she promised.

Elizabeth shook her head firmly. 'Not you. Mary said not to trust you.'

Amanda frowned.

'Her,' Elizabeth clarified, glancing nervously at Robin. 'Only her.'

Amanda handed her jacket to Robin, who held it out. Elizabeth wrapped it around her to cover her modesty, in part.

As suspicious as Robin was, she was kind. Amanda still wasn't sure how she felt about her, and she would still run that background check when she went back to work. But it seemed obvious that she wasn't out to hurt her. However she got her information about Amanda, it didn't seem like she meant her any harm.

'It's okay, love,' Robin murmured. She wrapped one arm around Elizabeth, and with the other, held Amanda's hand. She wasn't sure which one of them Robin was speaking to— maybe both—when she said, her voice soft as gentle as ever, 'I've got you. You're safe now.'

DESCENDANT

A woman desperately searches for answers, to figure out if her ancestor was, in fact, a witch.

Please note: this story contains spoilers for **The Pannell Witch**.

1

DINNER

Camilla pushed open the door to the restaurant and glanced around nervously. She inhaled the fragrant scent of fresh spices and saw a man in a smart black suit heading towards her.

'Good evening,' he said with a polite nod.

'Yes,' she nodded, letting out a groan as she dropped her heavy bag onto the floor. 'Table for one?'

'Of course. Follow me,' he said, with a kind smile. He spoke with a northern accent—it wasn't strong, but he was clearly from around here. He led her to a small table by the window. The restaurant was bathed in deep blue lights, with a candle on each table. It wasn't ideal for work, but it would do.

She glanced around the restaurant, pleased to see it was mostly empty. 'Actually, is there any chance of pushing these two tables together?' Camilla asked. 'I was planning to get some work done.'

The man smiled, doing as she asked without hesitation. He had soft brown skin, was probably in his thirties, like her. His eyes were wide, a shade of light brown that was almost translucent. He wore his hair long, but slicked back neatly. 'May I bring you some poppadoms?' He asked. 'While you work on your...' He trailed off, seemingly not wanting to push her for answers.

'I'm doing some research for a book,' she said, pulling a stack of papers out of her bag. She set them on the table and then sat down. 'And yes, please.'

'You're an author?' He asked, his eyes brightening. He handed her a drinks menu.

Camilla shrugged, the tops of her cheeks turning pink. 'I hope to be, one day. If all *this*—' She gestured to the mess of papers on the table. 'Pans out. I've been collating my research for a long time—it's only recently that I've found anything specific.' She ran a finger down the wine list, trying to figure out if she liked the sound of any of them.

He peeked over to look at the papers and hesitated at the copy of an old copy of 'The Leedes Intelligencer', from 1754. 'Your book is set in the local area, then?'

'Not exactly,' she said, handing back the menu. 'Just a glass of house white, please.' She held up the newspaper. 'This is the earliest newspaper I could find, but my book is actually about a woman who lived a century earlier.'

He raised an eyebrow. 'How interesting,' he mused. 'I'll be back in just a moment.'

When he was gone, Camilla spread out her research and started sorting it into piles. Everything that concerned a place she wanted to visit while she was here in Kippax went into one pile. Witness accounts of witches and ghosts went into another pile. The last pile included anything else— from artefacts she had collected, to articles about similar legends in the neighbouring towns. She wrapped a large elastic band around each of the second two piles and put them back into her bag.

The waiter returned with a basket of poppadoms, balancing three pots of dip in the other arm, and a large glass of cool white wine.

'Thank you, Aditya,' she said, glancing at his name badge.

'Please, it's just Adi,' he told her, tilting his head. 'What may I call you?'

'I'm Cami,' she said, taking a sip of wine as she surveyed the drawing in front of her.

'Wow,' Adi breathed, gesturing at the drawing. 'Is that your work?'

The paper was thin and discoloured, the edges ripped. Camilla had glued it to a piece of cardboard in an attempt to preserve it, and faded as it was, it was clear that it was an exquisite picture of a small hut in the foreground, with an old manor house in the background.

Camilla choked out a laugh. 'I wish. No, I believe this was the work of my—of a woman called Agnes. She will have drawn it before she got sick.'

'You think it was drawn from life?'

'I used to think so,' she murmured. 'But I haven't been able to identify it, and I doubt a hut like this would have survived until today.'

Adi smiled and tilted his head to the side like he knew something, but didn't offer up anything else. 'May I take your order?'

She gave it to him and spent some more time studying the picture.

He returned a moment later and held out his phone for her. It showed a large manor house, but the picture looked old—it was in black and white, and it looked like a sketch rather than a photograph. At least three stories high, the walls were light in colour and it had turrets on either side. It had evidently been expanded since Agnes drew the picture, but there was no mistaking the likeness.

'Where is this?' Camilla asked immediately. 'This is it! I've looked everywhere. Where is this place?'

Adi grinned. 'It looks different nowadays, but I think the place you're looking for is Ledston Hall. It's haunted, you know.'

Camilla scoffed. 'Oh, really? You're one of those?'

He shrugged. 'There are plenty of eyewitness accounts. You shouldn't turn your nose up at them. Why should you know any better?'

She rolled her eyes. 'You think there are ghosts in Ledston Hall?'

'I believe strange things have been observed in the area surrounding Ledston Hall,' he clarified.

'Mmhm,' Camilla sighed.

'Well, I suppose that's the setting of your drawing, anyway. The hut must have been somewhere in the surrounding fields.'

Camilla nodded. 'I know the hut is unlikely to have survived, but Ledston Hall could be crucial for my research. That does *not* mean that I believe in ghosts.' She hesitated, looking up at the man. He had kind eyes, and he seemed eager to help. 'It's not exactly busy in here tonight,' she said.

He smirked. 'Thank you. My parents will be pleased to hear that.'

'Sorry,' she said, her cheeks turning pink. 'I just meant— could I possibly convince you to sit with me? I'll buy you dinner,' she added quickly.

He rolled his eyes. 'I'll see what I can do.'

'Thank you,' she told him with a wide smile.

He returned with Camilla's order, along with an extra couple of dishes. 'Okay, Cami,' he grinned. 'I'm off the clock.

I'll help you with your research, if you agree to explain it to me. And you must agree to remain open to the possibility of ghosts.'

Camilla hesitated. Of course, it made no sense for ghosts to actually be a part of Agnes's history, but if agreeing to be open to it meant that Adi would help her, she was willing to try it. 'Fine,' she muttered. 'You're interested in this sort of thing, then?'

'I'm a local history buff,' he confirmed. 'I actually used to run a historical walk around here.'

'You must know a lot about the area. And its ghosts,' she said, her tone sarcastic.

Adi shrugged, ignoring her tone. 'So where did you find the picture?' He asked, picking up Agnes's drawing and running his fingertips over it.

'It's just a photocopy,' Camilla said. 'The original is hung on the wall in a London pub.'

Adi set the picture down and served Camilla some rice and dhal and then served himself. 'She was talented,' he said, taking a bite. 'Do you think she sold her drawings for a living?'

Camilla shrugged, sorting through the other sheets of paper. 'It's hard to say. But none of these other drawings are complete, and they seem to be all done by her.' They are sketches of people and places, but covered in rough lines and some of the faces aren't quite filled in. 'I like to think she would have done, if she'd lived longer,' Camilla finished, a hint of sadness coming through her tone. She put down the pictures and ate some of her curry. 'This is delicious, by the way.'

Adi smiled. 'Good.' He picked up a large map, faded in places.

Between bites, Camilla gestured to it. 'That's from the

1620s. It was produced when a fayre came to West Yorkshire.'

Adi nodded, running his eyes over the map. 'Do you want me to show you the place in the drawing?'

'Adi, I hope to God you're being serious.'

He choked out a laugh. 'Like I said, local history is a hobby of mine. I know this place well. And you obviously know quite a bit—I'd like to see what we can figure out together.'

'Me too,' Camilla said eagerly.

'It's quite famous, actually, that hill. We call it the Mary Pannell.'

Camilla's head snapped up in shock.

'What?'

'Mary Pannell was Agnes's mother.'

Adi raised an eyebrow, like he knew something, but it was unclear what it might be.

They finished their meal without figuring out anything else, and agreed to head up to Ledston Hall afterwards, to see if they could find any information to help with Camilla's research. Although Adi seemed intent on scaring her with ghost stories.

2

LEDSTON HALL

'This way?' Camilla asked Adi.

'Yep,' he said. 'Careful you don't slip.' It was almost pitch black now, with no streetlights anywhere near them. The grass was damp, and there was a light pattering of rain coming down on them.

'Did you used to do your walks up here?'

'Sometimes,' Adi said.

'Ever see any ghosts?'

He paused, taking a few more steps before answering. 'You really shouldn't joke like that.'

'Don't tell me you're offended.'

'I just don't think it's helpful to make fun of other people's beliefs.' He walked on ahead.

'Hold on,' Camilla called out. 'Don't just run off—look, Adi. I'm sorry. I didn't mean that, I promise.' She caught up to him, but he didn't turn to face her.

He adjusted his heavy backpack, gripping the straps firmly, and trudged up to the top of the hill, Camilla close behind him.

Ledston Hall was pretty, but in a sort of eerie way. It

seemed odd to her that there was so little movement around here. She would have expected there to be numerous cars running to and from the house, or even people walking the grounds, perhaps walking a dog. But there was nobody else.

'It's quiet,' Camilla said.

Adi sighed. 'Maybe the people were scared off by the ghosts.'

She grabbed him by the wrist. 'Please,' she begged. 'Would you just listen? I'm sorry, truly. I won't be rude about anyone's beliefs. I'll listen. I promise.'

The lights from Ledston Hall lit up his face, and his features softened. 'Fine,' he allowed. 'Listen. Ledston Hall has been privately owned for centuries, but the owners are almost never here.'

Camilla frowned. 'The lights are on.' Not all over the house, but there were certainly lights coming from some of the windows. The house was taller than she had imagined, and although it was behind a set of imposing stone gates, she could still see through. Behind the gates was a drive—though it looked more like a car park, a circular expanse of gravel.

He shrugged. 'It'll be the staff.'

'Won't we get in trouble? If they find us here?'

Adi's lip curled up into a smile. 'Better stay quiet, then,' he said, leaning against the wall. 'Let's see your picture, then.'

Camilla took it out of her bag, and Adi lit it up with the torch on his phone. 'We must be close by,' she said.

Adi looked from the picture up to the grounds of Ledston Hall. 'I think the hut must have been this way,' he said. 'Let's go.'

Camilla frowned. She wasn't sure what good it would do to find the exact spot of the hut, but she didn't see the harm in it either. And she *had* promised to be open to all this. 'Fine.'

They made their way over to an oak tree that was visible in Agnes's picture and appeared to be not far from Ledston Hall. Its leaves gave some shade to the space near the hut. 'Do you see a river anywhere?' Camilla asked him.

'A river?'

'The Lin Dike,' she clarified. 'I think it ran along the space right by the hut.'

Adi's face brightened. 'This way.' He hurried over to a small ditch. There was no water there, but he explained that there used to be. During times of year when it rained a lot, it filled in, but it was often dry.

'How do you know all these things about this area?' Camilla asked.

'Ah,' Adi grinned. 'My family goes way back.'

'Your family is from around here?'

'Don't look so surprised. My father was born and raised in India, but my mother's side of the family has lived around here for centuries.'

Camilla sighed as she glanced around the seemingly empty expanse of grass. 'I'm not sure why you think we'll find anything here.' She batted his hand away when she felt it on her left shoulder. 'Stop it,' she warned.

'Stop what?' Adi's voice came from her right-hand side.

Camilla's head snapped up. She frowned. 'Nothing,' she murmured. 'I must have imagined it.' A chill surrounded her, but to be fair, it was late, and they were standing in the middle of a field.

'Right. Well, follow me. I want to show you something.' Adi knelt down on the grass and patted the ground, moving his hands around.

She followed suit, feeling around for something. 'What are we looking for?'

'A flat stone,' he said. 'It's engraved, but only faintly.'

Camilla couldn't find anything but damp mud and when a particularly spiky weed cut her hand, she let out a yelp and sat back on her heels. 'And you've seen this before?'

'Not personally,' he admitted. 'But I've read about it. It's supposed to be out here somewhere. They say a relative should be able to find it.'

'A relative?'

'Mmhm.'

Camilla tried to figure out what he was talking about. 'You said your mother's family has lived around here for a long time.'

'I did,' he confirmed, not bothering to glance back up at her.

She rolled her eyes. 'So what exactly is it that a relative should be able to find? And why do you care so much?' A whistle sounded behind her, and she whipped her head around, but there was nothing there.

'It's a grave,' Adi said quietly. 'They say the witch who was burned on the Mary Pannell was buried somewhere here, in this field.'

Camilla frowned, confused. 'You mean Mary Pannell?'

He shrugged. 'I've never seen any convincing evidence that it was Mary Pannell who was killed here.'

'You think someone was killed in her place?'

'I think that if we find her grave here, we'll have the answer to that. It must be around somewhere.'

She looked at him, wearing a curious expression half-hidden in the darkness. 'Well, if that's true, why hasn't anyone found it? Surely the technology exists to find a grave.'

Adi sighed. 'It's not that the technology doesn't exist, Cami. It's that people don't care.'

Camilla brushed the dirt from her hands against her thighs. 'What do you mean?'

'My ancestor came to this country from India,' he told her. 'Look.' He took out his phone and navigated to a folder, opening an image. 'You can zoom in. It shows how you can trace my family all the way back to a woman who lived in this place. Mother Pannell.'

Camilla did zoom in, and was surprised to see just how far the family tree went back. Her eyes caught on a name just below Mother Pannell. 'She was Mary Pannell's mother?'

'No, but they were close,' Adi said. 'They weren't related by blood, but by marriage. Mother Pannell was a well-known medicine woman in the local area. Helped the whole community to treat their ills. It is said that she passed on her knowledge to Mary, so that she could continue to help the community.'

Camilla tried and failed to stifle the scoff that left her lips.

He raised an eyebrow. 'You don't believe me?'

She hesitated. 'I don't believe that people knew anything about medicine in the 1500s,' she clarified.

Adi took back his phone and navigated to another picture. 'You see this?'

Camilla looked at the image, this time of a leather-bound book.

Adi scrolled across slowly, showing a series of photographs of the inside of the book. It was a mess of pages slotted in, and falling out, filled with scribbles and images, many of the pages too stained to be visible.

'What about it?'

'It's a record of the remedies Mother Pannell used. It's held in the local museum—they found it in Ledston Hall years ago.' Adi smiled widely. 'And the medicines—they work. Some of them are even used by doctors to this day.'

Camilla frowned. 'But how did she know—'

'I think she brought the knowledge with her from India,' Adi said. 'Either that, or she picked some things up on her way to England. It would have been a long journey, and she would have travelled through a lot of places, full of diverse kinds of people, before she ever arrived here.'

'Let's just say Mother Pannell *is* buried here,' Camilla said slowly. 'What exactly are you looking for?'

Adi sighed. 'I'd like to find her grave. Uncover it, if possible. The woman who was burned for witchcraft in 1603 deserves to be remembered.'

'I mean, this whole area is named after Mary Pannell.'

'And yet, nobody ever talks of Mother Pannell. I don't even know her first name.'

'You seem so sure that Mother Pannell was executed here, not Mary Pannell,' Camilla mused.

Adi shrugged. 'It's just a feeling, I suppose. Mother Pannell's blood runs through my veins. And I feel like she wants her story to be told.'

'What story?' Camilla insisted, still not sure what he was getting at.

'It's my belief that she sacrificed herself for Mary. That she was executed in her place, because she wanted Mary to go on and have a full life.'

Camilla stared back at him. If this were true, it would certainly be noteworthy.

'This whole town knows the story of Mary Pannell, or what they think is her story,' Adi said. 'All I want to do is find out the truth. To find out if Mother Pannell was not only

Mary's mentor, but her protector. It's important to me,' he added quietly.

Camilla looked at him for a moment. She considered the depth of his determination. If anyone was going to find this grave, it would surely be him. She shrugged. 'I'm not going to stop you,' she said.

Adi went back to searching the ground for the stone.

Camilla scrolled back through the images to find the family tree, pausing when she saw 'Agnes Pannell'. 'That's her,' she murmured. 'She was Mary Pannell's daughter.' The woman she had come here for. Her ancestor. 'Agnes.' The name slipped off the tip of her tongue, and at that moment, she heard the whistling again. She snapped her head up and saw a figure heading towards them. 'Look,' she said, pointing at it.

'Hold on,' Adi muttered. 'I think I've found it.' He scraped away a layer of mud, digging his fingernails into the dirt.

'Fuck,' Camilla breathed. 'Who *is* that?'

The shadowy figure wasn't quite visible in the darkness, but by its silhouette, it appeared to be wearing a dress.

Camilla jumped to her feet and ran after the shadowy figure.

'Stop!' Adi called after her.

But she ignored him. She headed blindly into the distance. The wet mud meant her feet squelched into the dirt as she ran. She got closer and closer. But in the dark, the face was hidden. Finally, she got close, and she narrowed her eyes to try to see who it was. But it disappeared. A chill brushed past her ears and she shivered.

'No luck,' Adi called out. 'What are you doing?'

'Tell me you saw that.'

'Saw what?'

Something clicked for Camilla, and she dropped to her knees. She frantically started digging into the ground with her fingers. 'I think it's here,' she breathed. The ghostly figure had led her to this spot.

In a moment, Adi was there, too. Helping to get through the layers until the dirt was brushed away. Until there was a cold, flat surface of stone.

She handed Adi his phone and took out her own as well. They both shone their torches on the gravestone, on which, exactly as Adi had said, the letters were mostly faded. But they were certainly there.

'There,' Adi said. 'That says 'Panal', right? I'm not sure about the spelling—'

Camilla felt a jolt in her chest. 'That doesn't matter,' she said. 'Back then, they rarely had standard spellings for names. And not everybody could read or write, anyway...' she trailed off, running her fingers over the impossibly old stone. 'I think Agnes is buried here,' she murmured. 'And she's not alone.'

'Fuck,' Adi breathed. 'She led us here. She led *you* here, Cami, for a reason.'

They spent a long time trying to figure out the last name on the gravestone, and the dates. Eventually, they uncovered the inscriptions.

Here lies Agnes Panal, 1575-1603, beloved daughter and sister

"Mother" Salima Panal, 1517-1603, trusted wise woman of Kippax and beloved mother

'Agnes was twenty-eight when she died,' Camilla gasped. 'That fits. That's right when she left London.'

'Her name was Salima,' Adi breathed, staring at Mother Pannell's grave. 'She was eighty-six, and was buried with Agnes.'

Camilla felt around the area for another grave, but didn't find one. 'Mary's not buried here.'

Adi nodded. 'I knew it. The stories were wrong. It wasn't Mary Pannell who was executed here, but Mother Pannell. And Agnes Pannell's body must have been transported here, too.'

Camilla needed to know more. Here was her ancestor's grave, from over four hundred years ago. In that moment, she vowed to find out what had happened to Agnes Pannell.

CAMPING

A group of teenagers, adamant they are not scared of ghosts, go camping up on the Mary Pannell to prove it.

But when they come across Mary, their secrets start to unravel.

1

CAMPING

Freddie groaned, leaning over his girlfriend and trying to take the lighter from her. 'Would you let me do it?' Their tents were up, but it was getting cold, and soon it would be dark. He had no desire to be stuck in the woods with no source of heat or light.

'Why are you so irritable today?' Alice asked, pushing him away with her hip. 'Hold on, I've almost got it.' She held the kindling close and watched as the flame engulfed it.

'I'm not,' Freddie insisted. He sighed. 'I'm fine. Can we talk about something else?' He met her eye, and she nodded, but said nothing. Neither of them did for a long while.

Their two friends called back from the trees, but Freddie couldn't quite make out their words. He walked around his and Alice's tent, stepping on the pegs to make sure they were pressed deeply into the ground. There were heavy clouds overhead and if it was going to rain overnight, their tents would need to be watertight. The others' tent wasn't pulled as taut, and some of their guy ropes weren't attached to pegs at all. Freddie rolled his eyes. Not his problem. He reached into his tent and pulled out his and Alice's sleeping mats, setting them by the fire, one on top of the other, and then he sat on them cross-legged.

Alice glared at him from across the fire, sitting on a pile of twigs. Her skirt rode up slightly on her hips.

The other two came tumbling out of the woods, laughing about something. Both Freddie and Alice scowled at them.

Luna's face lit up. 'Alice! You lit our fire?'

The tops of Alice's cheeks turned pink. 'Yep,' she said, popping the 'p' like she always did. In that way that always annoyed Freddie.

Luna knelt on the damp ground next to Alice and spoke to her in hushed tones that Freddie couldn't quite hear.

Xander threw a pile of firewood to the ground and sat on the mat next to Freddie. He sighed, resting his elbow on Freddie's shoulder. 'We saw her,' Xander said, a glint in his dark eyes. Xander's mess of black hair fell down the sides of his face in loose waves. His skin was dark and smooth and his lips were wet, the light from the fire shining on them in the early evening.

Freddie cleared his throat and looked into the flames. He took a stick and used it to rearrange the wood, to protect the centre of the fire from the wind, and then he added one of the logs that Xander had brought over. He glared at Alice, who had stopped tending to the fire, in favour of whispering about something to Luna. 'Saw who?' Freddie sighed.

Xander shoved him until Freddie turned to face him. 'Mary,' he murmured, unable to hide his grin.

'Oh my *god*, you're an idiot,' Freddie muttered.

'I am not.' Xander's smug smile brightened his expression.

'You realise ghosts don't exist, right?'

Xander rolled his eyes. 'That's not true. My aunt saw my grandfather, years ago. Long after he died.'

'I know that's what she *says*,' Freddie said. He was all too used to the stories Xander's aunt loved to tell. 'She's the one who always goes on about Mary Pannell, too.'

'That's true.' Xander raised an eyebrow, as if daring Freddie to challenge him.

'Didn't she claim to have seen her when she was a kid?'

Xander smirked. 'And now I've seen her, too.'

'Fuck off,' Freddie said, pushing him away. 'And get off me.'

Xander moved his arm and reached over Freddie to the cool box they'd brought with them. 'Who wants a beer?'

'Yes please,' Luna smiled sweetly, finally looking away from Alice.

Xander passed the girls each a beer and then took two more, handing one to Freddie. He sat back down next to him, thighs close but not touching. 'Anyway, Luna saw her, too. Didn't you?'

'Sure did,' Luna said without hesitation. Her expression gave no indication of humour, like she was being dead serious. 'I was just telling Alice about it.'

'You're all crazy,' Freddie sighed.

'What is wrong with you tonight?' Alice asked.

Freddie scoffed. 'What are you on about?'

'You're so fucking moody, I don't even know what I've done. I just—'

'Hey, hey,' Luna interrupted. 'Let's keep it civil. We're all here to have fun, okay?' She took a gulp of her beer and met Alice's eye. 'Let's play a drinking game.'

Freddie groaned, glaring at her.

'Yes!' Alice squealed, excitedly.

Xander nudged his knee into Freddie's. 'You are not

allowed to be moody all night,' he murmured. 'The least you could do is drink with us.'

Freddie rolled his eyes. 'Fine.' His knee was still touching Xander's.

'Never have I ever?' Luna asked.

'Ugh, I hate this one,' Freddie sighed. But the others didn't seem to have heard him.

'Stop being so moody,' Alice scolded him. 'I'll start. Never have I ever got so drunk that I couldn't remember how I got home,' she said, smirking at Xander.

'I am not ashamed.' Xander shrugged and sipped his drink, though none of the others did.

'Never have I ever wanted so badly to not play this game,' Freddie glowered, draining his beer.

Xander shoved him, his fingertips brushing his bare shoulder. 'Fuck off,' he teased. 'Or I won't give you any more to drink.'

Freddie shivered at his touch. A wave of warmth spread from his shoulder, where Xander's fingertips touched him, right down his arm. 'Fine,' he murmured.

Once again, Xander leaned right over Freddie to the cool box and pulled out two more ice cold beers. The ice from the box had almost all melted, and when he sat back down, he paused when he was kneeling up, holding them over Freddie's lap. He dripped icy water all over him.

'Oi,' Freddie groaned. 'That's fucking cold.'

'Sorry,' Xander said with a smirk, not looking in the least apologetic. He brushed off Freddie's jeans, as if he could wipe away the water soaked into them like it was dust.

Freddie didn't tell him it was pointless, he just let him run his hands down his thighs, without meeting his eyes.

'My turn,' Luna smiled. 'Never have I ever had sex in a tent.' She glanced around, and when nobody drank, she ran her tongue along her top lip. 'Mm,' she hummed. 'Not yet, anyway.'

Alice and Xander burst out laughing at that, at the implication that later on Luna and Xander were going to have sex right there, but Freddie just grimaced. Things between Freddie and Alice hadn't been great recently. In fact, he couldn't even remember the last time they'd kissed properly. Somehow, they never found an opportunity to be alone together anymore. When they had first got together, they grasped any opportunity they could to sneak off into a broom cupboard at school, or send a quick text to the other if their parents were going to be out for a couple of hours. The likelihood oft hem having sex later on that night was small, no matter what Luna and Xander were doing in the other tent. He pushed the image right out of his mind. That was the last thing he wanted to picture.

'I'll go next,' Xander said, running his fingertips around the rim of his beer bottle. 'Hmm, never have I ever...' He hesitated, lost in thought.

The stubble that covered his face was thicker on his upper lip and on his chin than it was on his cheeks. Freddie couldn't help but think about how it would look if he ever grew it out.

'Ah!' Xander cried, making Freddie jump out of his ridiculous daydream. 'Never have I ever kissed a boy.' His gaze went straight to Freddie.

Freddie's cheeks heated. Why was he looking at him like that?

Xander glanced pointedly to Freddie's beer, held stock still in his hands.

Freddie gave a brief shake of his head, pleading silently to talk about something else.

Xander shrugged. 'Just us then, girls,' he grinned, holding up his beer.

The girls clinked theirs with him, giggling as they all drank together.

Freddie's mouth went dry when he realised what that meant. He stopped listening and didn't even hear what Luna said on her turn. All he could do was think desperately through the boys at school, trying to work out which of them Freddie might have kissed. Their faces ran through his mind, but none of them seemed quite right.

'Oi,' Alice said, throwing a bottle cap at him. 'I *said*, never have I ever thought ghosts were fake.'

'For fuck's sake,' Freddie sighed, taking a drink.

Xander did, too. 'To be fair, I used to think my aunt was fucking insane.'

Luna leaned in over the fire and lowered her voice to a whisper. 'Why? What did she tell you?'

Xander smirked, shooting Freddie a look that made him *ache,* before leaning over as well, his face inches from Luna's. 'Terrifying ghost stories,' he whispered back.

'Never have I ever believed a ghost could hurt me,' Freddie couldn't help but say, his voice sharp, pulling the others out of whatever trance they seemed to be in.

Xander pulled his face away from the fire and drank. 'What?' He asked when he saw Freddie's expression. 'I'm not ashamed. Ghosts see *everything.* If you piss one of them off, they could do whatever they wanted to you.'

'You're so full of shit.'

'Come on, have you ever actually heard a real ghost story?' Xander asked.

It seemed the game was over, as Luna had crawled almost onto Alice's lap, and Freddie focused on Xander. He was looking right at him, a glint in his eye.

'I've heard plenty of ghost stories,' Freddie insisted, scowling at the girls. 'But they are exactly that. Stories. Fiction. They never happened.'

Xander grinned. 'Sure they didn't.'

It was getting dark now, and other than the fire lighting his face from below, there was nothing but darkness all around. The rustling of the wind through the leaves was the only sound other than Xander's exaggerated breaths. Freddie watched his neck as he swallowed, his Adam's apple bobbing in his throat. 'Fine,' Freddie murmured, the disdain gone from his voice. 'Go on. Let's hear one.'

He raised an eyebrow and set down his beer. 'You all want to hear?'

Luna grinned from her spot on Alice. 'Definitely.'

Xander launched into an explanation of a woman accused of witchcraft in the 1500s, when her only crime was being a lesbian.

Freddie scoffed, warming his hands over the fire. 'There's no way you could know that for sure.'

'No? You don't think so?' Xander asked.

Alice rested a hand on Luna's back and shrugged. 'I think she was definitely into women.'

'She was married, to be fair,' Xander said.

'She may not have been opposed to men, but she definitely has queer energy,' Luna said with a wide smile.

'People used to be so afraid of women expressing their sexuality that they would end up believing the oddest things,' Alice added.

Freddie rolled his eyes. 'How exactly would someone back in the 1500s have expressed their sexuality?'

'She lived with a woman, you know.' Luna smiled. 'They say Mary lived with a woman called Elizabeth from when her husband died until her death.'

'Maybe they were just—'

'Friends?' Alice scowled. 'Yeah, thanks for that. Such an original thought.'

Luna rubbed Alice's back and spoke softly. 'Alice, he's right. We don't actually know what her relationship with Elizabeth was like.'

Freddie shot his girlfriend a smug smile. 'Told you.'

'Fine. But it's not a lie to say that at that time, people were threatened by people who were different. There are plenty of stories about women in relationships with other women who were ignored or persecuted, but never outright,' Alice said.

'That's true,' Xander added. 'My aunt told me that homosexuality in women was never actually illegal in this country. Many people even believed it didn't happen. That women couldn't even be gay.'

'But when it did, they accused them of witchcraft,' Alice said. 'Or at least, people were more suspicious of them. They used to hate any woman living successfully without a husband. They were weaker, and often were targeted by those in their communities.'

'Mm,' Xander hummed in agreement. 'We don't have any surviving court records for Mary Pannell, so we don't know exactly what the witness statements from her friends and neighbours said, but we do know they found her guilty.'

Freddie met Xander's eye. 'Guilty of witchcraft?'

'Exactly,' he said. 'She was well known in the community for the herbs and remedies she mixed up to treat various illnesses.'

Alice grimaced. 'That makes it even worse. She was accused by the very people she made it her business to help. And all because she loved another woman?'

'She was also poor. She was a servant to the Witham

family, and she was an outsider—she lived in a small hut in Kippax, just outside the main part of the town. So we don't know that she was targeted, accused, *convicted* because of her sexuality,' Xander mused.

There was a pause, and Luna gazed towards the trees. 'Sometimes you just get a feel for these things.'

'You're talking rubbish,' Freddie sighed, gulping down his drink. His mind was going delightfully hazy, despite his foul mood.

'She looked gay to me,' Luna said, slurring her words slightly as she leaned back against Alice.

'How the fuck could a ghost look gay?' Freddie sputtered.

Alice glared at him. 'Not like you would know.' As soon as the words left her lips, her eyes widened. Like she hadn't meant to say that aloud.

Freddie frowned, hesitating for a moment. 'Fine,' he sighed.

'What?' Alice asked.

'Let's go. Let's go and find the ghost, see if she seems gay,' Freddie said, finishing the rest of his drink and throwing the bottle to the ground. He jumped up to his feet and, without waiting for the others to follow, headed straight into the trees.

Footsteps ran after him and Xander's laugh ran through his mind. It took Freddie a moment to realise that he wasn't imagining it. That he was right there, passing him another beer that he definitely did not need.

'You hear how stupid that sounds, right?' Xander asked, leaning his elbow on Freddie's shoulder as they walked along together.

Freddie didn't shake him off. He found that his touch grounded him, even as he could feel the haze of the alcohol spread through him. He leaned into him as they made their way deeper into the expanse of trees, until eventually, Xander had his arm draped over Freddie's shoulders.

They were quiet for a long time, until eventually Xander squeezed Freddie's shoulder and leaned in to whisper right into his ear, 'did you hear that?'

Freddie whipped his head around. There was a quiet rustling of leaves, but louder than he would expect than if it were only because of the wind. 'Was that you?' He asked his friend.

Xander raised an eyebrow. 'I've been here with you this whole time,' he said.

Of course he had been, but Freddie still didn't believe that the noise could be anything to do with a ghost. 'It is *not* Mary's ghost,' Freddie insisted in a whisper.

'Let's find out,' Xander grinned. He slid his arm from Freddie's shoulder and tiptoed through the trees, taking care to step onto exposed rocks or fallen tree trunks wherever he could. It minimised any sounds of cracking branches or rustling leaves underfoot.

Freddie's face fell, disappointed at the loss of contact. He crept after his friend, oddly eager to see what was making the noise. He was sure it would just be a fox, or maybe a rat.

But for some reason, he felt a thrill of excitement thrum through him when he saw Xander hide behind the tree trunk of an old oak tree. Xander's hand reached out to pull him over to join him.

He inhaled sharply as Xander pressed him up against the tree trunk. They both faced a small clearing where the sound had been coming from, Xander's chest close against Freddie's back.

Xander whispered into Freddie's ear, 'fuck, look at them.'

Freddie realised then that he hadn't been looking at

anything. He had been focusing only on the closeness of his friend, on the sound of his breathing.

But right in front of them were Alice and Luna. Their arms were wrapped around each other, making soft moaning sounds as they licked into each other's mouths. Luna's hand was sliding dangerously low down Alice's back, and she was making no effort to stop her. The wet smacking of their lips had both of their boyfriends staring, entranced, until Xander span Freddie around, slamming him against the tree trunk.

Freddie stared back at him, wide-eyed. 'What are you doing?' He mouthed. No sound came out, but Xander grinned, like he had read his lips.

'What do you think I'm doing?' Xander asked, smirking as he leaned in.

But that was too much for Freddie. The haze that filled his mind cleared, and he pushed him away. 'Stop it,' he hissed. An emotion bubbled up inside him, something like anger. The image of his girlfriend kissing another girl was rooted in his mind. That was not acceptable. How could she do this to him? He shoved Xander away and pulled out his phone, pointing it towards the girls.

They were still making out, and Luna's hand had now disappeared down Alice's skirt.

'You can't fucking—' Xander tried to grab Freddie's phone from him, but Freddie pushed him away again.

He pressed the button to record them.

Xander reached up again, but Freddie held him back, holding his phone up high, on the other side of him. 'You can't take a video of them when they don't even know,' he hissed.

Freddie scoffed. 'I can do what I want,' he whispered,

angling his phone down slightly so both of them were in shot. 'She's *my* girlfriend.'

'Mate, this is fucked up,' Xander whispered, screwing up his face. 'What are you even planning to do with the video?'

'If she tries to deny it, it's proof,' Freddie said, his words slurring into one another. He had the moral high ground here, and he was not going to let Xander convince him otherwise. 'Proof that she's cheated, and that I know about it.'

'What the fuck do you need proof for?' Xander huffed. 'There won't exactly be a court case, prick.'

'Fine,' Freddie mused, his mind going through the other possibilities. 'Maybe I'll send it around. I could post it online. Make life really fucking difficult for her.' There was a tone of such disdain in his voice that he didn't even recognise.

Evidently, Xander didn't, either. Because he stepped back, glaring at him.

But before he had the chance to explain, to take it back, a cold gust of wind made him shiver. In a second, he was pushed over, and he landed on the floor.

Freddie let out a scream, a burst of terror flying through him. It felt like an animal had rammed into him, and he pictured some kind of deer with long, sharp antlers heading straight for him. He'd hardly be able to fight back, and he'd end up speared on those antlers, with Xander and the girls running away, back to safety.

He was lying on his stomach, his mouth full of dirt, and he turned his head, groaning, to see what was to blame for his fall. There was no sign of an animal. There was no evidence of any creature at all, and Freddie spat out a mouthful of—he didn't even know what—into his hands, before throwing the mixture to the floor. He ran his tongue along his teeth and grimaced.

'Fuck!' Xander shouted, grabbing him by the wrist. 'Don't swallow.'

The girls pulled away from each other and came over. 'What are you two doing? Were you *watching*—' Luna began, but Xander interrupted.

'Please, Luna. Not now.'

Freddie frowned. 'What are you on about?' He asked, his mouth still full of dirt.

Xander pointed to the ground. 'See those toadstools?' He asked.

On the ground, mushed up from being shoved into Freddie's mouth, was a pile of brightly coloured mushrooms, as far as he could see. 'Shit. Are they poisonous or something?'

'Extremely,' Xander said, reaching into his backpack for his bottle of water. 'Swirl your mouth out with this. Do not, under any circumstances, swallow.' He rooted through his bag, trying to see what else he had that might help.

Freddie did what he was told, rinsing his mouth out.

Xander handed him a mini bottle of mouthwash and a pack of gum, and Freddie shot him a grateful look.

'This is so weird,' Alice said, watching as Freddie tried desperately to remove all traces of the poison from his body. 'You were hiding out in the bushes, watching us? And then you accidentally fall into a pile of poisonous mushrooms?' She glanced over at Luna. 'Is this meant to be a joke?'

Freddie spat mouthwash out onto the forest floor, then ran his tongue along his teeth to make sure all traces of the poisonous mushrooms were gone. 'What exactly would the joke be?' He asked. He popped some gum into his mouth, desperate for the fresh, clean taste in his mouth.

Alice's cheeks turned red, but she didn't respond.

Instead, she stepped closer to Luna, who wrapped an arm around her.

That was just about too much for Freddie to take. He grabbed his girlfriend by the wrist and tried to pull her away from Luna. 'Get off her,' he muttered.

Alice's eyes widened in fear at his touch.

'Take your hands off her,' Luna almost growled at him, her voice low and angry.

Freddie was barely aware of what they were talking about. The haze that filled his mind confused everything. All he knew was that he was mad at his girlfriend, and he wanted to get her *away* from Luna as soon as possible. He didn't release her.

Xander's eyes narrowed. 'It's not funny, mate,' he said. 'If you don't let go of her right now—'

Before Xander could finish his sentence, Freddie felt it again. That cold gust of wind, shoving him back onto the cold ground. He moaned and tried to roll back around, to see which of his friends had done it. He deserved it, he supposed. But in his drunken state, he just wanted to speak to his girlfriend.

But a foot held him there.

'Oi, Xander,' he mumbled into the ground. 'Can't breathe. Let me up,' he pleaded.

He heard hushed voices, but the foot didn't let up. The surrounding air was icy, but maybe that was just because he was on the ground.

'Seriously,' he breathed, but his face was pushed into the ground again. He was starting to panic. Okay, he had acted like a prick, but these were his *friends*. They wouldn't actually hurt him, would they?

More murmurs sounded around him, like they were

close, but there was some kind of barrier muffling them, so he couldn't make out the words.

He closed his fists at his sides, dirt seeping into his fingernails. 'I'm so—' again, he struggled to get the words out. 'Sorry,' he managed, his breaths now loud and laboured.

There was a scream right above him. A girl's scream. Alice's. He pictured her face. The beautiful curves of her cheeks and the dimple on her right side when she smiled only for him. *I'm sorry*, he thought, as his thoughts melted away into nothing.

'Look,' a boy's voice said, panting. 'Did you see that?' Xander. It was Xander.

'He definitely flinched,' Alice said in an oddly high-pitched tone.

Freddie blinked his eyes open gradually, and it was dark. He was lying on the cold, damp forest floor on his back. Above him, towering over him, was Xander.

A wave of relief spread across Xander's face when Freddie broke into a coughing fit, pushing himself up to a seated position.

'That's it,' Xander murmured, coming around to stroke his back. 'There you are.' He smiled sadly.

'Wha—where was I?' Freddie asked, confused. Why was Xander looking at him like that?

Alice took his hand and squeezed it. Her eyes were wet, her cheeks puffy. 'Fuck, you're okay.'

Guilt filled him when he saw his girlfriend and remembered what he had done. 'Alice, I'm sorry. I'm so, so sorry. I was angry, I wanted to get back at you—'

'It's okay,' she breathed, cupping his cheek.

'It's not,' he grimaced. 'I didn't mean to...' He trailed off. How was he supposed to explain that he hadn't meant to grab her? That he had barely even realised what he was doing? It wasn't *him*. Didn't feel like something he could do. He had never raised a hand to a partner and he couldn't understand what had made him do it in that moment.

'I know,' she said simply.

'And you and Luna,' he began, eager to clear the air if it was at all possible. 'I'm sorry I got so angry.' He wasn't against her being with Luna if she wanted to be, but he was hurt. He'd made a rash decision and wanted more than anything to take it back. All that went unsaid, but he hoped she would understand his meaning.

'You were filming us,' she said.

He scrunched up his face. 'Fuck, I know. I don't even know why I thought that was a good idea.'

'Me neither,' she admitted.

'What?' Freddie asked, confused.

She pulled a face. 'I, um—I knew you were there.'

Freddie glanced over at Luna, who was watching them closely, kneeling down a few steps away from them. 'When you kissed her?'

Alice nodded. 'I wanted you to see. Wanted to make you angry.'

Freddie sighed, pulling away from her hand. This wasn't the way relationships were supposed to be. He was turning into a fucking awful person, and he was ashamed. None of this was who he wanted to be. She deserved so much better than him. He hesitated before saying quietly, 'this isn't working.'

She bit her lip and nodded, meeting his eye. 'I know.' He had always felt like he knew her so well, until recently. But looking at her now, it seemed like he knew her once more. Like she had opened up her thoughts to him again, and he wasn't afraid of them.

'Come on, mate,' Xander said, awkwardly pushing Alice off him and helping him up. 'None of this, okay? It's depressing.'

He shrugged, smiling at Alice. 'I don't think it is. I think we've been broken up for a long time. But maybe now we can move on.'

She gave him a knowing look and, in that moment, he knew she understood. 'Come on, Luna,' she said, taking her hand. 'It's late. Let's go to bed. I don't think Mary's ghost is angry anymore.'

Freddie watched them walk away and frowned at Xander. 'Mary's ghost?'

Xander smirked. 'How else do you explain what happened?'

'It was you!' Freddie insisted. 'You had your foot— holding me down—' But even as he said it, he realised it couldn't have happened that way.

Xander would never hurt him. And whoever had pressed him down into the ground kept his friends from helping him, cut off his breathing until all the air left his lungs—they were not his friend. Xander looked at him, tilting his head as if he were trying to figure something out.

'Sorry,' Freddie murmured. 'That was stupid of me. I know you wouldn't.'

Xander pulled him into a hug and patted his back firmly. 'Course not,' he said, laughing awkwardly. He held him for a little longer than might be expected, and when he spoke again, his voice hitched. 'We're mates.'

Freddie pulled away slightly to see that Xander's eyelashes were wet. Those long, dark eyelashes that batted back at him. Those eyes, staring right into his own. Without stopping to think about what it might mean, without taking a moment to consider what the consequences would be,

Freddie pressed his lips against Xander's. Xander melted into his touch, his arms wrapping around him, hands gripping his waist. His lips parted and their tongues met, easily sliding against each other like they had been doing this all along.

The kiss lasted a long time, and when Freddie finally was the one to pull away, he was delighted to see that Xander's lips were wet and glistening in the moonlight. 'Thanks, Mary,' Freddie whispered, and he leaned in once more.

MOTHER

Anyone who sees the ghost of Mary Pannell is cursed.
Doomed to soon lose a member of their own family.

So the legend goes. But Kathy is determined to prove that
she is not afraid of an old ghost story anymore.

This story contains some potentially upsetting themes.

1

WOODS

Kathy made her way along the path in the low light of early evening, wrapping her cardigan tightly around her. She huffed as her son jumped into a particularly deep puddle. 'Leo!' she called. Muddy splatters dirtied his white t-shirt.

But he didn't take the time to glance back at his mum, apparently too excited at the prospect of finding even deeper puddles to splash in.

'He's a nightmare,' Kathy sighed. It was windy, and her normally perfect hair was blowing about in front of her face. She grabbed the hair clip she always kept in the front pocket of her handbag and twirled her perfectly coiffed blonde hair into its grip. 'And what is with the weather today?'

Eve was less concerned with keeping her hair neat, and simply let it fly wildly about. She grinned, nodding at her own son, who appeared to be nervously watching Leo. 'Ah, it's cute. And look—I think Noah wants to play, too.'

'Leo!' Kathy called. 'No running off. Stay with Noah.' Her son ran back and whispered something to him.

Noah shot him a shy smile and bounded off after him, stepping through the puddles after Leo jumped in them.

Kathy turned back to Eve and rolled her eyes. 'Sorry. He gets so distracted, he ends up running off by himself.'

'Oh, it's nothing. Noah dotes on him,' Eve insisted. 'Honestly, he's been so worried about starting school—but as soon as I told him Leo would be starting there, too, he suddenly *wanted* to go.'

Kathy smirked. 'Those boys are going to be best friends for a long time. I can feel it.'

'We'll make sure of it,' Eve said, hesitating for a moment. Their sons were out of earshot now, though they could still easily see them in the field up ahead. She lowered her voice in concern. 'How are you doing, really?'

Kathy adjusted her handbag on her arm and cleared her throat. 'I'm doing fine.'

Eve sighed, slowing her pace when she saw Kathy was slowing down. 'Don't think I haven't noticed. You've been late to work every day this week, and you haven't joined the rest of us for lunch at all.'

'No, that's not—I mean, I'm not—' Kathy started.

'I'm not trying to intrude,' Eve interrupted. 'But you can talk to me.' Her voice was steady, calm. She never pushed, but still, Kathy often found herself revealing parts of herself when they spoke. Eve was kind and put you at ease. It was one of the things that made her such an excellent nurse.

Kathy bit her lip, thinking over the past week. It was true that she'd been late to the hospital a lot. Every day might be pushing it, but she had certainly not been her usual self recently. 'I know,' she murmured.

'How are things with Alan?' Eve asked, going straight for the heart.

Kathy screwed up her face. 'He moved out,' she admitted

quietly. She kept her eyes on the field ahead, on her son, who was too young to understand the difficulties his parents were facing. 'He's having Leo this weekend, and I think he's going to stay involved as a father, no matter what happens between us.'

'Mmhm,' was all Eve said.

Kathy let out a low groan. 'I don't want to talk about it.'

'I won't argue with that,' Eve said, the corner of her lips curling up into a slight smile. 'I haven't been married in what—five years? And I can't say I miss it.'

Kathy wished she could be so sure that she was better off divorced. But she really didn't want to talk about it right now. Tucking a loose strand of hair behind her ear, she asked, 'so, why did you want to walk up here today?' Kathy had become quite used to spending time with Eve, who had moved up north a year or so ago, and they got along easily. But generally, when they spent time together, it was a play-date at one of their houses.

Eve raised an eyebrow, her dark eyes glistening like she had a secret. 'Have you been up here before?' She asked.

Kathy frowned. 'Of course. I've lived in Kippax all my life.'

'Not just here, in these fields,' Eve clarified. 'There, in the woods.' She pointed over to the Mary Pannell, just across the main road.

'Fuck, no,' Kathy blurted out, fear laced in her voice.

'No?' Eve said, her tone light and teasing.

'Ugh,' Kathy groaned. 'Someone's told you, haven't they?'

'Oh, don't tell me you're afraid of ghosts.' Eve scoffed, crossing her arms as she got closer to the main road.

Leo was standing right at the edge, staring right into the woods.

'Leo!' Kathy shouted.

Eve called out to her own son. 'Noah! Not so close to the road. Wait for Mummy.'

Noah grabbed Leo's shirt and pulled him away from the road.

'Get back here, Leo,' Kathy ordered, though her son didn't come back. Both boys waited at the main road for them.

Once their mothers got there, they each took their son's hand and waited for the road to clear. There were lots of cars racing down the road and it was loud.

'I don't know about this,' Kathy said, glaring at the trees. 'It's getting late, too.'

Eve frowned. 'It's not late, it's just that summer's over, so it's very slightly darker than you're used to.'

'Exactly,' Kathy told her. 'It's dark, and that means it's dangerous. Especially for the boys.'

'The trees aren't that thick,' Eve insisted. 'And it won't actually be dark for hours. We'll be able to see fine. Let's just have a brisk walk around, and then we'll walk back?'

Kathy ran her free hand through her scalp, frustrated. 'Why are you so desperate to go in there?'

'Haven't you ever wondered if it's true?' Eve asked.

Before Kathy had a chance to answer, there was a gap in the traffic, and Eve led Noah across the road. Kathy and Leo followed.

'Mum,' Leo groaned, trying to pull his hand away.

'Leo, stay safe,' Kathy told him, squeezing his hand. 'If I let you go, you're to stay close. If you can't hear me talking to Eve, you come back.'

'Yes, yes, yes,' he muttered, jumping from foot to foot, eager to explore the woods.

'And *stick* with Noah. Promise me?' Kathy asked.

'Promise,' Leo said, meeting his mother's gaze.

'Good boy,' she murmured, kissing his hand and letting him go.

Leo and Noah didn't go too far. At first, they tried to climb up a tree with some low branches, but neither of them could quite reach high enough.

'It's not true,' Kathy said, sighing as she watched the boys.

'What's not?' Eve walked slightly ahead of her, and when she had almost caught up to the boys, they got bored with their tree and ran off up ahead, chasing each other through the trees.

'The legend. There is no way Mary Pannell haunts these woods.'

Eve rolled her eyes. 'If you really believe that, why haven't you been here before?'

Kathy refused to answer her. She watched her boys through the trees, and when she felt an icy chill brush the side of her exposed neck, she screamed out for her son. 'Leo?' A shockwave of pain shot down her neck, through her whole body. Like she could *feel* that something was wrong. That someone else was there with them. Watching them.

A hand pressed on her waist, and she almost jumped out of her skin.

'Kathy, it's me,' Eve murmured, stroking her back softly.

Kathy turned to see that Eve was just behind her, looking at her with a curious look in her eyes. 'Oh,' she said, confused.

'Are you sure you're alright?' Her friend asked her. 'You sort of... tuned out for a minute there.'

All around her, the woods seemed to have darkened. They were now surrounded by trees, and although she could still see the boys up ahead, kneeling down and rooting through the leaves, she felt disoriented. 'I, uh—sorry. I thought I felt someone.'

Eve frowned, taking her hand away. 'You mean me? I was just checking on you.'

Kathy hadn't been getting much sleep recently. She was sure that explained what she had felt. 'Yes,' she lied. 'You startled me, that's all.'

They walked in silence after that. Kathy hoped that would be the end of it, but she was still on edge. The chill she had felt, the hand on her. It wasn't Eve.

'I'm thinking about getting back into dating,' Eve said eventually.

'Oh?' Kathy tried her best to sound interested, but her mind was elsewhere. And her eyes were fixed on her son.

'Actually, I've been talking to someone,' she admitted. 'He was a bit pushy at first, so I thought—'

A figure appeared ahead. The outline of a woman. Kathy was fucking *sure* of it. 'Did you see that?' She gasped, pointing at it.

'See what?' Eve scoffed. 'I was just saying—'

'There,' Kathy insisted, speeding up to try and catch whoever it was. They had disappeared into the dark expanse of trees. 'Will you watch the boys?'

'What?' Eve asked. 'Where are you going?'

The flowy hem of a white dress poked out of the bushes, and Kathy raced after it. She ignored the calls of her son behind her and ignored the shouts of Eve behind him. Roughly pushing the branches aside, not caring about the scratches left on her arms, she found her way along a path that had long overgrown, and followed the rustling up ahead of her. She caught more glimpses of the dress, and was convinced this was a woman running away from her. 'Stop,' Kathy called, panting. 'Where are you going? I'm not here to hurt you.' But still, she chased after her. For curiosity's sake, maybe. Or perhaps she just wanted to prove that this figure wasn't a ghost. That she *wasn't* going crazy.

She eventually found her way into a clearing. It wasn't dark anymore. Hot flames fanned up in front of her face, under an immense pile of logs. A pyre. Kathy was standing in front of a massive pyre, on top of which lay a body. A woman's body, clothed in the same white dress she had followed through the trees.

Behind her there was a scream. A child's scream. One that was eerily familiar.

'Leo?' Kathy shrieked. She turned away from the fiery flames and ran back in the direction of her son's scream. In her hurry, she tripped over a branch on the ground. A layer of skin on her palm ripped when she tried to break her fall. But she got up, kept going. 'Leo!' She cried when he didn't call back to her. The trees all looked the same, and it felt like she was never going to find her way back to where the sound had come from.

'Kathy?' Eve called.

Kathy ignored her friend—she needed to find Leo. Now. There was no ghostly figure to guide her now. She was helpless but to run around aimlessly, desperate to catch any glimpse of her son.

The edge of a rough line of rocks made her stop in her tracks. Even in the dark, the moonlight shining through the trees, she could see the sharp edges. The puddles glistening in the light, slippery. Kathy's heart sank. She knew what had happened before she even saw it. It was like she felt it.

Still, she somehow made her feet move forwards, advance until she was at the edge. It wasn't far down, but that wouldn't have mattered.

Leo lay there, at the bottom of the small hill, his body

twisted awkwardly on the ground, blood flowing quickly from a head wound. Soaking the ground underneath. Crimson stains seeped through his white t-shirt, cruelly covering him more and more by the second.

'Kathy!' Eve called again, closer this time.

Kathy burst into action, jumping down into the ditch she hadn't seen there before. She tore off her cardigan and wrapped it tightly around her son's head, before holding a hand in front of his mouth.

He wasn't breathing.

She checked her watch and began chest compressions immediately, and called back to Eve. 'Call an ambulance! He's not breathing, so I've started CPR.'

'Shit, shit, shit,' Eve muttered, her voice carrying down to Kathy.

But Kathy didn't have the mental capacity to say anything else, to focus on anything else. She didn't listen to Eve's offers to take over, or respond to Noah's sobs when they floated down to her ears. She focused only on her boy. On Leo. On doing whatever the fuck it took to bring him back to her. As exhausting as it was to continue with the chest compressions.

Sweat dripped down her forehead and time seemed to move without her even realising, because a paramedic was suddenly next to her, spitting out words she didn't want to listen to.

'What?' Kathy snapped.

A young man kept his voice calm, but quick. 'When did you start CPR?' He asked. Concise, to the point.

'7:25pm, I started,' Kathy confirmed. She checked her watch again. Fuck. It had been twenty minutes. 'I'm a nurse. I started as soon as I found him.'

'Let me,' he said, taking over from her. His colleague appeared then, holding a box out to him.

'Got the defib for you,' she said.

'Cheers,' he said, letting her set up the pads, sticking one on Leo's upper chest, one on his lower chest, while he continued the compressions, kneeling over him. Towering over him, small as he was. 'So how long after he fell down here did you find him?' He asked, his voice a little breathless.

Kathy bit her lip. She hadn't thought to check the time when she'd heard him scream. 'Fuck,' she muttered. 'Um, not long. Maybe a couple of minutes?'

He didn't respond to that, but he stopped CPR when the other paramedic was ready with the AED.

Kathy didn't bother to listen to the stupid automated voice recording. She just watched, tuning out all the other sounds, as Leo's tiny body jumped up in the air, agitated by the surge of electricity. She watched, tears streaming down her face, as she pleaded silently with whatever god might exist to please bring her boy back. To give her back her son.

But it was all for nothing.

Leo didn't start breathing again.

Kathy felt like she may as well not be breathing anymore, either.

2

AFTERMATH

In the days after Leo's death, Kathy wasn't quite herself. She was aware of time passing, of friends and colleagues popping in to check on her, but it was all sort of fuzzy. Like a dream. Not real.

Eve was there a lot. She brought her food, and without her, Kathy might not have eaten at all. She certainly wasn't thinking about herself at that point. The only image in her mind was that of her son, of that t-shirt soaked in blood. Of his head wound wrapped up in her own cardigan. Of those never ending chest compressions that had all been for nothing.

Memories came to her in pictures. In soundless re-imaginings of time spent with Leo. She saw him grinning at her from across a room. Stamping his feet in frustration when he couldn't get his shoes on. Jumping in muddy puddles that dirtied his clothes. Every single memory took her back to that place. To those woods she had never visited as a child. She had avoided that place because something deep within her had known what would happen. Some part of her had always felt there was something to the stories.

She hated herself. Despised herself for not listening. After all, legends all started somewhere. They don't just come into being from nowhere. The stories of Mary Pannell had haunted this place for hundreds of years, but Kathy had thought herself above all that. She had thought herself immune to the risks, and for what? For a walk through the woods with a friend? For a quiet evening playing outside with her son? They could have simply stayed in the nearby fields, and none of this would have happened. Her life would never have been torn apart so brutally. She would have her son back.

The funeral passed by in a blur. She was only vaguely aware of family and friends surrounding her. They shook her hand, whispered soft comforts in her ear. Or, they whispered what they thought was comforting, anyway.

Alan was there. At least, Kathy thought she saw him. The first time she saw him, he had tiny little Leo in his lap. He was bouncing him, and Leo was giggling. Part of her knew that he had never laughed before. That this was the first time. But that didn't make sense. That happened years ago.

Dishes of food were set out on a long table, and someone brought a plate over to Kathy, shoving it in her hand. 'Eat something,' the voice said. She looked up, and this time, Alan's face was different. His hair was shorter, like it had been cut, and his wrinkles were more pronounced. His rage was clear in his darkened eyes, his pursed lips. This must be the real Alan, she thought. The Alan that had also lost a son.

She spooned mouthfuls of tasteless sludge into her mouth until the gaze of those around her seemed to relax. For endless hours, she sat there, waiting for the crowds of people to leave. To leave her to wallow, to sort through her own mind. To figure out what the hell she was supposed to do now.

Alan was the last person to leave. Kathy stood at her front door, trying to tune out his voice, but he reached his hands to cup the sides of her face, and shook her. 'Kath, listen,' he urged.

She swallowed, coming back to reality for a second. Meeting his gaze, she noticed his eyes were red and puffy, his beard coming in, even though usually he preferred to be clean shaven. Even his shirt was creased. He wasn't looking after himself any more than she was looking after herself. 'What?' She asked, the word coming out more harshly than she intended.

'It's the autopsy,' he murmured, dropping his hands. 'I know what they told us, but it just doesn't make sense to me.' He lowered his voice, glancing around as if to ensure nobody else would hear him. Though there was nobody there. 'You said he fell, but then why wouldn't they have shown us their results? I don't think this was an accident.'

Kathy shook her head, trying to figure out what he was saying. She leaned back against the doorframe, unable to support her own weight anymore. 'Wait, Alan,' she said, narrowing her eyes. 'You know I would never—'

He waved a hand in dismissal. 'Yeah, yeah. I know. Of course it wasn't you. But you didn't actually see him fall, right?'

Kathy hesitated, and when the words left her lips, they were barely a whisper. 'I heard him scream.'

'Exactly,' Alan said under his breath. 'I think someone pushed him.'

'You—what?' Kathy asked quietly.

Alan nodded, as if this were simple, stepping closer to

her. 'He used to run around places like that all the time, never once did he fall. He was pushed. He must have been.'

Kathy flinched. She didn't want to go back to that place. 'Stop it,' she whispered.

'No,' Alan huffed, raising his voice. 'I won't stop. My boy is dead, Kath.'

'Stop it,' she begged, stepping back into the house. 'Please.'

'Kath,' he growled. 'I'm not letting this go. This is not over.'

Kathy pushed him away and slammed the door shut in his face. She had no desire to look at him anymore. When she was finally alone again, she turned and leaned her back against the door, before sliding down until she was sitting on the floor. She buried her head in her hands and sobbed. There were no tears left, but the dry sobs wracked her brain, emptying it of any and all rational thought.

3

ACCIDENT

When Kathy was finally getting more than just a couple of hours of sleep a night, she started to feel like herself again. The first thing she did was to clean. Her house had got messier and dirtier since everything had happened, and although she hadn't used the kitchen for cooking, that was where a lot of the rubbish had ended up. Any of the meals Eve had brought over had been dumped in there, half eaten. Takeaway boxes littered the kitchen worktop, and the bin was overflowing.

Kathy took out the rubbish, swept the floor and wiped the worktops clean. It was then that she spotted the pile of post wedged up against a bottle of wine. Glancing at her watch, she saw it was still morning, but it wasn't like there was anyone here to judge her. She opened the screw top and chugged down a gulp of the warm white wine, wincing, but enjoying the glide of it down her throat all the same.

She grabbed the pile of envelopes and the bottle of wine, and headed back to the lounge to plop herself down on the sofa and go through the pieces of her shattered life. There were a lot of cards passing on others' condolences. Friends, colleagues and neighbours, even some people she was sure she had never heard of were telling her how sorry they were. The cards had pretty pictures of flowers, of people hugging. One of them had written that Leo was in a better place, and Kathy ripped the card into four pieces immediately, throwing it on the floor.

Gulping down some more wine, she turned to the other envelopes. She ripped open a serious looking one and found that it was from the hospital. They told her not to worry about coming into work for the next few weeks, that they would arrange for some cover. She scoffed. She was hardly worried about work right now. The letter said they would be in touch at a later date to discuss a date for her return to work. This one again, she threw to the floor. She went through more letters, and more wine, until she came to the last letter.

It was from the local police department. It explained that while there were some anomalies with the autopsy, Leo's death had been ruled an accident. There was not sufficient evidence to charge anyone with harming him, and although she was welcome to request a copy of the autopsy report, it would not affect their decision. The letter ended with condolences and was signed off by an officer whose name Kathy did not recognise.

She stared at it, trying to take the words in. Accident. Not sufficient evidence. Autopsy report. A minute later, she had grabbed her phone and dialled the number in the top right-hand corner of the letter.

The phone rang for a long time before a tired sounding man picked up.

'Yes, hello. I'd like to request a copy of the autopsy report for my son,' Kathy said, not wishing to waste her time with pleasantries.

'Uh, yeah. Okay, let me just—'

'Now, please. I don't have all day.'

The man cleared his throat. 'Apologies, ma'am. I have to advise you that we can't simply provide copies of documentation during an ongoing investigation—'

'It's not,' she interrupted him.

'Oh?' He yawned.

Kathy gritted her teeth. Where was this man's sense of urgency? 'Please. The investigation has been closed, and I received a letter saying that I am free to request a copy of the report.'

'I see,' he murmured, the sound of his keyboard tap-tap-tapping in the background. 'In that case, erm, do you have a case number?'

Kathy scanned the letter and found it. 'Yes, it's JC26594. Could you email it to me?'

He sighed. 'No can do, I'm afraid, love. It's post only.'

'Could you please just make an exception?' Kathy asked, her voice coming out in a desperate whine. Now that she had finally gathered the energy to do something, she felt like she had to keep going. If she didn't, she was going to fall apart.

'Sorry, it's for security, you see,' he said, his voice softening slightly. 'Ah, this was Leo, was it?'

'Yes,' she snapped. 'Look, can you please ensure it goes to my correct address as soon as possible?' She read out her address clearly.

'Of course, ma'am. I apologise for your loss.'

She hung up on him. Fucking useless. Not that she expected anything more. Her next phone call was to Eve, but she didn't pick up. She was probably on shift. But this was more important.

Kathy hadn't showered, hadn't even brushed her hair

since she couldn't remember when, but she grabbed her keys and pulled on a coat. She reached into the shoe stand by the front door, but along with her own shoes, she pulled out a smaller one. A tiny white trainer, the blue parts faded with age. She stared at it, not wanting to put it down. Because if she was holding Leo's shoe, that meant he was still with her. Somehow.

But this wasn't the time for that. She put his shoe down and pulled on her own. She drove to the hospital with a one track mind, focusing only on the job she had set for herself. Alan had kicked it all off, she was grateful to him for that. She had already completed the next step—requesting a copy of the autopsy report. Until that arrived, she wouldn't know the extent of Leo's injuries as catalogued by the medical examiner. But there was another person there that day. Another nurse, who would have seen Leo's injuries close up. And she—hopefully—wouldn't have been quite as out of it as Kathy had been.

Kathy parked in her usual spot—there was no point risking her car getting clamped just to save a couple of minutes. She pushed through the familiar double doors and ignored the hushed murmurs of her colleagues as they watched her glide down the corridors. She knew if she asked someone where Eve was, it would spark an entire conversation about why she was coming back to work so soon. They would no doubt tell her to go home, to rest, that she shouldn't be out. So she would find Eve herself.

It didn't take long. Eve was pushing an old man in a wheelchair, and when she caught sight of Kathy, her eyes softened. 'I'll be just one moment,' she said, and she gestured for another nurse to come and take over.

'Kathy,' Eve said, wrapping one arm over her shoulders. 'Is everything okay?'

Kathy choked out a low laugh. What a ridiculous question. 'No, Eve,' she spat out, with more contempt than she had wanted. But she didn't take it back, and Eve didn't scold her for it.

Instead, Eve fixed her with a long look, her eyes flicking up and down Kathy's neglected body. 'Are you eating, pet?'

Kathy scowled. 'I'm fine.'

'I'm sorry I haven't been around in a few days,' she went on. 'I'll pop by tonight. How does that sound? Bring you over some dinner. You should go home, run yourself a nice bath—'

Kathy sighed. 'Please,' she tried, her voice cracking. 'Will you tell me what you saw that day?'

'I don't think...' Eve stroked her back and made a face. 'What you need is to talk to someone more qualified than me. You've been through an awful shock, and you shouldn't be out and about—'

'Eve!' Kathy shouted, standing up and pushing her hands off her. 'Just fucking tell me what I'm asking and I'll leave.'

Eve's eyes widened. But she nodded slowly, not even glancing around at all the people staring at them. They were in the middle of a busy waiting room, but paid no attention to the other patients or staff. 'Okay. What is it you want to know?' She gestured to the seat next to her.

Kathy sat back down. Eve was a good friend, really. She didn't mean to shout at her. But she couldn't bring herself to apologise. 'I need to know about Leo's injuries,' she said in a low voice.

'From when he fell?' Eve crossed her legs, and the look she gave her was pitiful, like she thought Kathy was about to break.

'Nobody saw him fall,' Kathy hissed.

'Oh, love,' Eve cooed. 'Is that what this is? Look, it's perfectly normal to feel this way. I think you should consider getting some grief counselling. The NHS offers it to their staff for free. I can arrange it for you if you like—'

'Please answer me,' she begged. Kathy was not interested in grief counselling. She had more important issues to focus on. Like Leo.

Eve sighed. 'I saw him bleeding out from a head wound. And...' She hesitated.

'What?' Kathy asked, her eyes widening. 'What else?'

'I'm not blaming you,' she said carefully. 'I think you were probably just scared when you found him. You were panicking. That's what I told the police.'

A lump formed in the back of her throat. 'What are you talking about?'

Eve made a face. 'The bruises. On his face and neck. He had fingerprints bruised into his fair skin, like—like someone had held him down, tightly.'

All the colour drained from Kathy's face. 'I didn't,' she muttered. 'It wasn't me.'

Eve let out another sigh. 'I don't blame you, honey. It was traumatic, okay? For me, too. Don't worry, though—I didn't mention it to Alan. And the police officer I spoke to promised me it wouldn't be a problem—he was already gone by the time...'

'What?' Kathy's head was spinning, trying to make sense of her friend's words. 'You're not listening to me.' She thought back to that day in the woods. About the other woman she had seen in the woods. The only other person who could have done this to her boy. The very woman that had led her away from her son in the first place.

'I know you didn't mean to hurt him. But you would never have actually pushed him. Anything you did was in an effort to save him.' Eve took her hand and squeezed it. 'I saw the anguish in your eyes when you realised he was gone. That's what I told the police. They said they would normally look into a case like this further, because of the bruising and the way he fell into such a shallow ditch. They were asking lots of questions. But I shut it down, okay? You don't have to worry about anything.'

Kathy groaned. 'No, no, no,' she muttered. 'This can't be —can't be happening.'

Eve tried to pull her into a hug, but Kathy pushed her away.

'It was her,' Kathy choked out.

Her friend stared back at her, shaking her head slowly. 'What are you talking about, love?'

'It was her!' Kathy repeated.

'Who?' Eve gestured for another member of staff to come over.

'She took my boy from me,' Kathy breathed. 'She took Leo.'

Eve shook her head. 'It was an accident, Kathy. Listen to me, this was not your fault. This was nobody's fault.'

Kathy nodded, the anger raging inside her. Because she understood. She finally fucking understood what had happened. 'It was Mary.'

Eve's eyes widened as she caught on to what Kathy was saying. To what she was claiming must have happened to her son. 'No, Kathy,' she murmured softly, as another nurse appeared at her side. 'There's no such thing as ghosts.'

4

HOSPITAL

Kathy's colleagues descended onto her from both sides, holding her arms down even as she tried to push them away. But they were well-practised in subduing unruly patients, which she supposed she appeared to be.

The only way to convince them not to hold her was to stop fighting back. She knew that. Logically, in her brain, she was fully aware of that fact. But it was instinct that wouldn't let her stop. She was fighting for her boy. For Leo. The longer they kept her at the hospital, the longer she'd be kept from finding the truth out about her son.

'Let me go,' she pleaded, trying to meet the eye of the nurse holding her left side. 'My son needs me.'

He glanced over to Eve and frowned. 'Isn't her son the one who...?'

'Yeah,' Eve said, keeping her voice quiet.

Kathy groaned. 'No, that's not what I mean,' she said, shaking her shoulders, trying to get them to loosen their grip. 'I'm not having delusions, for fuck's sake—'

'Don't get aggressive with the nurses, Kathy,' Eve warned. 'Just relax. Talk to me.'

'Ugh,' she said, throwing back her head.

The nurses lay her down on a bed, and while two of them held her there, Eve strapped her down. 'Just stay here for tonight, okay? I'll keep an eye on you.'

'Don't,' Kathy begged, when she saw one of the nurses coming over to her, holding a needle. 'Don't sedate me. I promise, I'll calm down. I'm not crazy—' she pushed hard against the restraints, and when the needle got close to her arm, she raised her voice to the nurse. 'Fuck off,' she hissed.

But that was the worst thing she could have said, because it only confirmed that she was going to keep being aggressive towards them.

'Where would you go, if you left here?' Eve asked, holding up a hand to stop the nurse from injecting the sedative into Kathy's arm.

'I need to find—' Kathy started, before biting her lip.

'Mary?' Eve asked gently. 'You're going to go and look for the ghost you believe is responsible for your son's death?'

Kathy held her gaze. Eve would know if she was lying. But if she told the truth, perhaps she would believe her. Perhaps she would help her. 'Yes,' she breathed. 'Please, Eve. Help me find her. Help me get justice for Leo.'

Eve sighed, a sad smile crossing her face. 'I'm going to help you,' she said. 'I promise.' She nodded to the nurse, and the needle pierced her skin, the sedative making its way quickly into her bloodstream.

When she started to come to, there were muted beeping sounds in her bedroom. Kathy blinked her eyes open slowly and frowned, confused at the odd environment. She was at work. An ache made her arms heavy, so she tried to lift them above her head to stretch, but found them stuck. She craned her neck and saw the plastic straps tied around her wrists, buckling her arms to the hospital bed.

The events from earlier that day came back to her. They thought she was having delusions. She was acting aggressively towards the staff and talking about Mary Pannell had only made it worse. Kathy sighed, trying to get her thoughts straight. She had to convince them to let her go. 'Excuse me?' She called to a nurse near the door.

The young woman jumped. 'Sorry,' she said quickly. 'How are you feeling now?' Her voice was familiar, but Kathy couldn't remember her name. She was new. 'Much better,' Kathy lied. 'Sorry about earlier. I haven't been sleeping and, well. I shouldn't have taken it out on you. On any of you.'

She let out a sigh of relief and nodded. 'Um, Eve went home last night, sorry.'

Kathy frowned. 'What time is it?'

'A quarter to nine,' she said. 'She'll be in soon, if you want to wait for her?'

Kathy took a deep breath. If she had been here all night, she really needed to leave, to get started on her research. And if she waited for Eve to get here, she might end up having to stay for longer. After all, no matter how supportive Eve claimed to be, she was the one who had put her here. She was the one who thought she was having delusions. Eve had been there, in the woods, but hadn't actually seen Mary. So it made sense that she thought Kathy was making this up. It's what any competent nurse would assume—Kathy knew that. But she also knew she had to get out of here.

'It's okay,' Kathy said. 'I don't mind if someone else discharges me. I appreciate all of your help.' She tried to keep her tone steady, so she'd think she was being sincere.

She went off to fetch her paperwork and check that it

was okay to let her go, no doubt, while Kathy was left alone. She stared up at the ceiling and took deep, calming breaths. If she let herself get worked up again, they'd never let her go. Instead, what would help would be to create a plan. To come up with something tangible that she could do to help uncover the truth.

It all came down to Mary, of that Kathy was sure. She remembered seeing her body burn on that pyre, could still feel the heat of the flames on her cheeks. But that wasn't how she'd thought Mary had died. In fact, she wasn't all that certain how Mary died at all, just that she was said to haunt the woods on that hill. Perhaps the next thing she should do would be to find out exactly what really happened to her.

Kathy was brought back to the present when the nurse returned with her discharge papers. She kept her tone light as she asked the questions disguised as small talk, which Kathy knew all too well were meant to deduce her mental state.

'Do you have any plans for the rest of the day?' She asked, her tone breezy, as she sat on a stool next to Kathy's bed, a clipboard on her lap.

Kathy shook her head. 'None at all,' she sighed. 'I think what I'll do is run myself a hot bath, to help me relax, and then maybe watch a film.'

The nurse exhaled, visibly more comfortable. 'That sounds lovely,' she mused, ticking a couple of boxes on the form. 'What film do you think you might watch?'

Kathy kept eye contact when she looked up, keen to show her she was calm and ready to go home. 'Good question. I'll probably rewatch an old DVD. Maybe one of my favourite musicals.'

'Ah, I love musicals,' the nurse smiled. She set down her

clipboard and made quick work of loosening Kathy's restraints. 'How are you feeling now?'

'Well rested, at least,' Kathy said. She was careful not to appear too cheerful—they would know that wasn't real. 'I just need some time alone, I think. It was too soon for me to be out, really.'

The nurse nodded, apparently pleased with that answer. 'Glad to hear it. I'll let Eve know we had a chat,' she said. 'I think she said she was going to pay you a visit later on, perhaps bring you something to eat.'

'Lovely,' Kathy said. 'Will you tell her thank you from me? For everything she's done.' She plastered on the most genuine smile she could manage at that moment, and thankfully, the nurse didn't know her well enough to see through it.

She helped her up off the bed, and headed for the door. 'Your clothes are on the stool just there,' she said. 'If you sign the discharge form and then hand it in at reception—'

'Thanks, I know the drill,' Kathy interrupted, shooting her an apologetic look. It was five minutes to nine now. She didn't have long.

'Of course,' she said, before leaving the room.

Kathy made quick work of getting dressed and leaving the hospital, eager to leave before Eve arrived. With a stroke of luck, she managed it, and after paying a fortune for parking at the machine, she drove out of the car park. Right by the exit, though, she saw Eve driving in on the opposite side.

Eve rolled down her car window and called out something to her, but Kathy pretended she didn't hear her, and instead waved goodbye, before driving off.

5

RESEARCH

Kathy was not an academic sort of person. Firstly, she didn't have the first clue how to research something, and this was important, so she didn't want to get it wrong. There was no one in her circle of friends that that did this sort of thing, either, so it wasn't like she had someone she could ask for help. But she was determined to find out more about Mary Pannell. As she drove along, she wondered if she had ever heard of a historical society, or any kind of organisation that might know more about her story. But she didn't have a clue.

It was only after she'd driven past the library that she realised that might be a good place to start. At the next junction, she pulled a U-turn and headed back towards the library. There was a free parking space on the road, and so she pulled up before making her way inside. She saw her faded reflection in the library door, and for a moment was shocked at the state of her messy hair, her creased clothes. But none of that mattered right now.

When she pushed open the door, a bell sounded, and a woman looked up from the reception desk. She didn't frown at Kathy's appearance, and she didn't make any nasty comments, for which Kathy was grateful. Until now, Kathy had never left the house looking anything other than perfectly coiffed and made up. But there was no time for that right now. She had to push through, for Leo.

'Good morning,' she called, smiling widely, as if she knew her. 'Do you need any help today?' She had long grey hair down to her mid back and wore a long dress with a floral pattern on it.

'Um, would that be okay?' Kathy asked, standing awkwardly in the doorway.

'Of course!' The woman said, her face brightening. 'Did you want to join the library? Or are you a member already?'

Kathy walked over to the reception desk. The librarian wore a name badge that said 'Linda'. 'Well, no actually. This is my local library, but I'm afraid I've never actually been inside,' she admitted.

'Ah, not much of a reader?' There didn't seem to be any judgement in her tone, but even so, Kathy felt defensive.

'I love to read, actually,' she said. 'But I do ebooks, mostly.'

'Of course,' she said. 'Is there a particular book you're looking for today?'

Kathy took a deep breath. 'Um, not exactly.' She glanced around. The library wasn't massive, so she wasn't sure she'd be able to help, but it was worth a try. 'I was hoping to do some research on Mary Pannell.'

Linda's lips twitched. 'You mean The Pannell Witch?' There was something about her expression. She looked excited.

'Yes, I—I think so,' Kathy nodded. 'I've heard the stories, of course, but I was wondering what parts of her story are actually true.'

'Mmhm,' she hummed. 'I'm something of an enthusiast when it comes to local history. There are a number of varied accounts, but what have you heard exactly?'

Kathy hesitated, not sure how much she should reveal. She knew that she didn't want her to think she was disturbed, or in need of any further hospital stays. 'I've heard that she haunts the woods up on the hill she's named after,' she murmured. 'And that, um—she harms children,' she added, a tinge of sadness falling across her expression.

Linda's eyes widened. 'I haven't heard that version of the legend in a long time.'

'Fuck,' Kathy muttered. 'But you have heard it?' Part of her had been hoping that she was mistaken. That nobody had ever claimed that Mary Pannell wanted to hurt any children.

Linda let out a long exhale and glanced around the library. There were only a couple of others here, a mother and her daughter. They were in the far corner; the daughter engrossed in a book. 'Come on, let me show you something.' She led her over to a small table where there was an ancient-looking computer and gestured for her to sit on the chair in front of it.

'Thanks,' Kathy said, not sure what she was about to see.

Linda logged in and opened a program. 'This is our newspaper archive,' she said. 'We have copies of several local publications, going back hundreds of years.'

Kathy's heart flipped. 'Do you have any articles showing how Mary Pannell died?'

'Ah, I'm sorry,' Linda said, shooting her an apologetic look. 'They didn't actually have newspapers back then. Mary was killed back in 1603. The earliest we have is...' She clicked through a number of files until she found what she was looking for. '1754.'

Kathy frowned, pushing back her chair. 'Thanks anyway,' she sighed. 'It's only Mary's story that I'm interested in, honestly. It's sort of a personal project.'

Linda spoke quickly. 'Mary's story was passed down orally, so we have various different sources, none of them particularly reliable, unfortunately.'

'I know,' Kathy said, a little irritated. 'Everyone used to tell slightly different versions of it, but I'd really like to find out which parts were true.' She stood up and glanced towards the door. 'I appreciate you trying, but—'

'Please,' Linda said. 'We don't necessarily have any first-hand records of Mary's own life—the court records are gone, and all we have are the parish records confirming her birth and death—but we have plenty of references to the hauntings.'

Kathy felt a shiver run up her spine and she span back to face Linda. 'Hauntings?'

Linda nodded. 'Deaths, said to be caused by Mary's ghost, who haunts the area,' she confirmed. 'It is said that if you are unfortunate enough to see her ghost, a member of your family will die that very day.'

A shiver stayed right there on her spine. This was it. This was the part of the legend she recalled as a child. The whole reason she had stayed away from that wretched place. She groaned at the memory of the woods, wishing she'd never stepped foot in there.

'Ma'am?' Linda asked.

Kathy shook her head, coming back to the present. 'Sorry,' she said, forcing a smile. 'I've been a bit out of sorts recently.' It wasn't a lie, exactly. More a sort of half-truth. Linda didn't need to know what Kathy had been through, and if she told her, she'd have to face yet another wave of sympathy. She couldn't do it. 'And it's Kathy, please,' she said, sitting back in the chair in front of the computer.

'Kathy,' Linda smiled, tucking a strand of grey hair behind her ear and leaning over the keyboard. 'If you select the dates you want here,' she said, clicking in a box. 'Then you can enter any keywords here.' She typed in 1700-1900 and 'Mary Pannell', but there didn't appear to be any results.

Kathy sighed.

'Give me a second,' Linda said, pausing to think. 'I know there are some old articles about this in here,' she muttered to herself. In another program, she brought up the Kippax parish records.

'Is this where you can find the record of Mary's birth and death?' Kathy asked. It was all handwritten and hard to distinguish.

'Uh huh,' Linda said, scrolling up to try to find the relevant page.

'You should sit,' Kathy said, moving out of the way. She would be no help for now. She sat next to her and looked over her shoulder anyway until Linda made a sound of triumph.

'Aha!' Linda exclaimed. 'Here we are,' she said, pointing at a few names. 'Look at all these different spellings of her surname.'

It was difficult to read, but there were different spellings of it peppered across the records. There had evidently been lots of them living in this area. 'Oh.'

'Excuse me?' A man called from behind them.

Linda jumped up and showed him to the check-out desk, putting his books through for him, wishing him a lovely day and coming back.

'Sorry,' Kathy said quickly. 'I'm keeping you from your job. I'm sure you have better things to do than this.'

Linda shook her head and gestured over to the check-out desks. 'Most people use the self-service desks, anyway. And if they need me, they can ring the bell or come and get me. Besides, it's my job to help the members.'

Kathy didn't bother to specify that actually, she wasn't technically a member, instead choosing to just accept the help, because she really needed it. She'd be lost without Linda to help guide her through the computer system.

'Let's try this,' Linda said, navigating back to the news-paper archive and clicking on 'Advanced Search'. She entered a few alternative spellings including 'Pannal, Pannall, Panel' and hit enter. This time, three results popped up.

Kathy leaned over, eager to see what had come up.

'I apologise,' Linda said with a smile. 'I'll leave you to it.'

'No, wait,' Kathy said. 'If you're interested, I'd really appreciate the help. I'd never have thought to check the old spellings of her name.'

Linda grinned. 'Well then,' she said, tapping her hands on her lap. 'What would you say to a cuppa?'

'I'd love one,' Kathy admitted, relieved to be finally getting somewhere. 'Milk, no sugar, please,' she told her, and clicked on the first of the three search results.

The Leedes Intelligencer

No. 1, Tuesday, July 2, 1754

Printed by Griffith Wright, in the Lower-Head-Row

Kathy noted down the date on her phone. She wanted to ensure she had a record of this. Of every family this had happened to. Scrolling down past an article about a large mining disaster, she found what she was looking for.

Boy, 5, Found Dead

'Here you are,' Linda said, setting down two mugs of tea on the table.

Kathy thanked her and pointed to the screen. 'Look, isn't this the earliest year you said you hold newspapers for?'

Linda nodded. 'That's right. I believe, actually, that this is the oldest one on file. And there we are.' She raised an eyebrow at the headline, reading aloud.

A mother has reported that seventeen years past, her young son, but five years of age, had an accident in the Pannal wood. She suspects dark magic may have been the cause.

Kathy scoffed. 'That's it?' She typed it on her phone, anyway.

Linda sighed. 'I'm afraid that before then, there wasn't much in the way of newspapers. Quite a few of these articles actually related to incidents from the previous years, and after such a long time, it would have been difficult to verify more than a couple of facts.' She took a sip of her tea and navigated back.

Kathy groaned. 'Look, they didn't even spell "Leeds" right. I'm not sure how much we'll be able to find in these articles.'

Linda smiled. 'Actually, that was the accepted spelling until around 1765, I believe.'

'Oh, right,' Kathy sighed. She was never going to get used to this.

'Here we are,' Linda said, clicking on the next result down.

Halifax Guardian

29 July 1843

She scrolled down until she found the relevant article.

Tragedy Befalls Beaumont Heir

On Saturday 22 July, the five-year-old heir to the Beaumont fortune fell to his death in the woods up on the old Panel hill. The Beaumont family has released a statement confirming that they are having the incident scrutinised by a paranormal investigator.

A lump formed in Kathy's throat. 'This is... almost identical to the first story.'

Linda sighed, pursing her lips. 'It looks that way. Both families believed their sons' deaths were caused by something... not quite natural. Let's have a look at the last one. Hmm, that's odd.'

'What?'

'This one isn't a newspaper. It was published by a certain Joseph Holmes, who was a brewer's chemist.'

Kathy wasn't altogether sure what that was, but she was certain it wasn't anything to do with journalism. 'Why would they report on children's deaths?'

Linda didn't answer, apparently too absorbed in the mystery of the article.

The Brewing Trade Gazette

1 June, 1885

A monthly journal devoted to the interests of brewers, publicans, wine & spirit merchants

Price 6d.

Kathy read over her shoulder, but none of the articles seemed to mention anything relevant, until Linda scrolled down right near the end of the article.

'Of course,' Linda murmured. 'I remember this now. It's here, look.'

Wine market

Every Sunday, noon 'til dusk

The Pannall Wood

Underneath this advertisement, there was a small note.

Due to the increasing reports of deaths of young boys in the area, we must ask that no children are brought to the market.

'Fuck,' Kathy inhaled sharply. 'Increasing reports?' Although it barcly told them anything, it still appeared relevant, so this, too, she typed on her phone.

Linda leaned back in her seat, rubbing her temples like she was in pain. 'We have no way of quantifying just how many deaths there were up to this point. Either they weren't reported, or the reports simply didn't survive.'

'But that's—it's not—this is ridiculous,' Kathy said. 'There must be some more information *somewhere*.'

Linda navigated back to the Advanced Search and increased the date range. 'We can look at more recent publications, but as you can imagine, nowadays, people are much more hesitant to believe in supernatural entities, and so the reports read slightly differently. She entered '1900-Present' in the date field and hit enter. She clicked on the first result.

The Football and Sports Special
"The Green Un"
Yorkshire Telegraph and Star
Every Saturday
No. 75Sheffield, Saturday, February 18, 1909

Kathy frowned. This was a sports edition of the newspaper, and would hardly tell them anything at all.

'Sometimes you find answers where you least expect it,' Linda answered the question that she hadn't asked. She scrolled down, trying to find whatever reference she could to Mary Pannell.

'Thank you for helping me so much,' Kathy said, her voice weak. 'I can't explain how important this is to me.'

'Mmhm,' she hummed in response, eyes still on the screen.

'Seriously,' Kathy insisted. 'I mean, I tried to talk to my friend about it. She's my best friend, really. She was even there when—anyway, I can't even tell you how utterly unhelpful her reaction was.' She thought back to lying, tied to that hospital bed, and scowled. 'I know she thought she was helping me, but I just—I wish she had just left me alone.'

Linda shrugged. 'Some people don't know how to help us. It's not necessarily their fault, but it doesn't mean we have to listen to them.'

'Thank you,' Kathy repeated.

She didn't respond, she just pointed at the screen.

Kathy leaned in to read and copy parts of a short article about the five-year-old son of a footballer, found dead in the same woods that Mary Pannell's ghost is said to haunt. It said he had died from a nasty fall while out playing with his friends, and that by the time his mother came to check on him, it was too late. 'I can't believe how similar these stories are,' Kathy said. 'Every single one is about a boy—either five years old or not specified—who fell to his death in the very same place.'

'Mm,' Linda said, wasting no time in continuing to the next article. She scanned it quickly and then made a face. 'From here on is where they get more... commercial.'

Illustrated London News

30 April 1932

Look at Yorkshire

Kathy scoffed when she saw what this one said. 'Is this trying to convince people to visit, *because* of the hauntings?'

Linda sighed. 'You wouldn't believe some of the things people are willing to risk, just for a close-up view of witch-craft or ghosts.'

The article relayed the myth of the Pannell Witch, that any who saw her would soon have a death in the family, and also gave a brief description of another local witch called Mother Shipton.

'Do you think people actually came from far away to visit? Despite the risk?' Kathy asked, incredulous.

'I know they did,' Linda replied sadly. 'People love a ghost story.' She scrolled down the long list of articles in the 1900s until she came across the more recent ones. There were a number about Kathy herself, but she scrolled back up slightly.

Kathy looked closely at the old librarian and saw something in her eyes that couldn't possibly only be the academic interest of a local historian. No, Linda seemed personally touched by these articles, and was wearing an expression so similar to Kathy's. It wasn't the pity etched on everyone's faces at the funeral, or at the hospital. It was a deep understanding. 'You know who I am, don't you?' Kathy said. It wasn't a question—as soon as the words left her lips, she realised the truth of them.

Linda turned to her, and her eyes were glossy, like she was ready to cry at any moment.

'Did you lose your son, too?'

'No,' Linda replied sharply. 'She took him from me.'

6

MARY

Kathy had found someone who was uniquely qualified and motivated to help her with her work, and she was relieved. Sorry, of course, but so damn relieved. Linda was in this too—Kathy wasn't alone anymore. And she wasn't crazy. She sat there with Linda as she relayed her story. Thirty-two years ago, Linda had been in a very similar position to the one Kathy found herself in right now.

She was having issues with her partner, and had brought her son to the woods in the hopes of cheering him up. He had always liked to climb trees, but until that day, she had stayed away from that place because of the stories. But after her son had begged, after he had told her that their next-door neighbour had been there lots of times with her own mum, Linda had relented.

It was her biggest regret, not trusting her gut, and the moment she stepped through the trees, she had known something was wrong. 'I told the police,' Linda said, her eyes full of tears. 'I told them I saw her, but they wouldn't listen.'

Kathy frowned. She hadn't even told the police about seeing Mary. To be fair, she didn't really have the presence of mind to relay the information at the time, and then afterwards, Eve's reaction hadn't exactly given her the confidence to share her story with them. She was too scared of being labelled as unreliable, as suspicious. And what good would it do, anyway? 'I'm sorry,' Kathy murmured.

Linda sighed and gestured to the computer, which had a list of articles from around thirty years ago. 'Here, you can read the articles they wrote about me. The whole town branded me crazy, said I couldn't look after my own son, and then refused to put the blame where it belonged, on myself.'

Kathy skimmed the articles and found that they said exactly what Linda said. They detailed how her son died, said that he was five years of age, and that the death had been ruled an accident, despite the suspicious behaviour of his mother. 'I'm not interested in reading what they said about you,' Kathy said. 'As far as I'm concerned, you and I are the same. You saw her that day, just like I did. And she took our sons from us.'

Linda breathed a sigh of relief, like she had been waiting for someone simply to listen to her, to believe her. 'It all goes back to her. To Mary.'

Kathy nodded. 'But why? Why would anyone make it their mission to cause the death of all these young boys? It doesn't make sense.'

'Have you ever heard the story about how she died?' Linda turned to face her.

Kathy gulped, remembering that awful pyre. 'I think they burned her,' she murmured, pausing for a second to correct herself. 'No, scratch that. I know they did. I saw it.'

'You saw it?' Linda asked, eyes widening.

'That day, right before I heard—' Kathy took a breath,

trying to stay calm. The pain was still new, like it had just happened. 'She was there, in front of me. She wore a white dress, and it hung down off the side of the pyre as she burned. I could—I could feel the flames. The heat. It was like it was going to burn my face.' She shivered and then looked up at Linda's blank face. 'You didn't see that?'

She shook her head. 'No, I um—I think I saw her trying to escape.'

Kathy tilted her head. 'Escape?'

'From that place,' she said. 'Ledston Hall? That's where I saw her, running as fast as she could towards the woods, screaming as if she was in pain.' Linda was watching Kathy closely. 'I always just assumed everybody saw the same thing.'

'Why would she be running from Ledston Hall?' Kathy asked, her heartbeat quickening, as if she was on the verge of figuring something out.

'Well, in some versions of her story, it is said she was a nursery maid to the children of Ledston Hall,' Linda said, her words running together as she sped up her pace. 'Oh my god,' she muttered. 'Let me check something.' She turned back to the computer and pulled up the other program, which detailed the parish records.

Kathy was lost again, utterly bewildered by the library's computing system, and by the sheer scale of information. How could they expect to find anything useful? 'We already checked these,' she huffed, frustrated. 'We need to find something from Ledston Hall. Records of servants, some-how?' She was thinking aloud, and she knew it made no sense. What sorts of records would have survived from the early 1600s to this day?

'Aha,' Linda said excitedly under her breath. She pointed to the screen, which showed not the Pannell family, but the Witham family. 'I can show you records of owner-ship of Ledston Hall that confirm the Witham family resided there in 1603, when Mary was killed.'

Kathy squinted at the screen, trying to read what it said.

Wm. Witham, died 1603

'Wait, so you think this could be—'

'William Witham, who lived in Ledston Hall, died the same year that Mary was executed for witchcraft. Hold on, let me just find...' Linda interrupted her, scrolling up until she found what she was looking for.

Wm. Witham, baptised 1598

'Fuck,' Kathy said. 'So he was probably five years old when he died.' Her mind was reeling, trying to figure out what all this could possibly mean. 'But she—that's horrify-ing. Are you saying you think she's some sort of serial killer? That she's obsessed with killing young boys in death, just as she did in life?'

'No, I'm not—no,' Linda said. 'If she really was employed at Ledston Hall, and it really was her job to care for the boy, I can't see why she would have hurt him. But if he died while under her care, it's possible the family were looking for someone to blame. Someone to take out their anger on.'

7

PLAN

'You are not seriously telling me you think a ghost is taking out her sick revenge fantasy on you?' Alan scoffed over the phone.

Kathy groaned over the hands-free in her car. 'Please, listen. I have evidence. And it's not just me. She's taking revenge on the children of Kippax. Any five-year-old boy she sees in Kippax, actually. I'm sure of it.'

Alan let out a long sigh, pausing before replying. 'Look, sweetheart. You've been through hell—we both have. No one should have to lose a child.' His voice hitched as he spoke.

'This isn't—no,' Kathy said firmly. She glanced over to the passenger seat, where Linda gave her a small nod of encouragement. 'I'm not just grasping at straws here. Don't patronise me. When I tell you I have evidence, I mean it. And we're not the only ones this happened to.'

'Who else?'

Linda inhaled sharply, but Kathy didn't chance a look at her. It didn't feel like he was ready yet, like he'd be open to listening to Linda's story.

'I found numerous articles in newspapers over the years,' she told him instead. Perhaps if he realised the sheer scale of the problem, it would make him listen. 'Not just recently, either. They go back hundreds of years, and people have always known that the ghost of Mary Pannell was behind it.' She turned off the main road, and found herself on a narrow country road, enclosed either side by tall trees, blocking out the sunlight.

'That doesn't mean—' he began, his voice cutting out slightly as the phone signal got worse. 'Just because some old newspaper claimed to report a sighting of a ghost, it doesn't necessarily imply that—'

'Will you just fucking hear me out?' Kathy interrupted, raising her voice.

Linda jumped next to her, a cry leaving her lips.

'Who was that?' He snapped.

'No one,' she lied. 'Well, it's just...' It was unusual for her to get angry, but this was important. She paused, and when Alan didn't say anything, she continued. 'I met another woman—another mother. She's been through the same thing. Mary took her son from her, too.'

'Kath,' he said, his voice low. 'This woman is not your friend. She's trying to convince you that Leo's death can be explained by a ghost. Think about it. It doesn't make any sense.'

'You're not listening,' she groaned, running her fingers through her hair in frustration.

'It's here,' Linda said, looking up from her phone and pointing to a barely noticeable dirt road coming up. 'Turn left.'

'Is that her?' Alan demanded, his tone cold. 'Stop trying to rope Kath into your crazy scheme. She's got enough going on right now.'

Linda glanced over at Kathy, who shrugged, giving her permission to speak. 'There's no scheme,' she said, her voice measured and calm. 'Mary took my son just like she took yours, and dozens before them. Likely more.'

He scoffed.

'You were suspicious,' Kathy said, stopping the car outside a dilapidated looking old farmhouse. It was a single-storey building made of stone, with smoke coming out of the chimney. 'Wasn't it you who said you didn't believe this was an accident?'

They all went silent and she and Linda shared a look.

'I didn't mean *this*,' Alan murmured. 'But just... I meant maybe he was pushed. I thought maybe someone had run off when you found him. There must be someone who's responsible for this. An actual human person. Someone killed our boy.' His voice hitched, like he was trying not to cry, and he cleared his throat.

An old man stood in the doorway of the old farmhouse, watching them both curiously.

'Eve rang me,' Alan admitted.

'What?' Kathy hissed. 'What would she have to say to you?'

'Don't jump down my throat. She's just worried about you, that's all.'

Kathy threw her head back against the driver's seat. 'She had no right.'

Alan sighed. 'She said the police suspected you at first. Her, too. That must have been very difficult to deal with.'

She wasn't about to humour him. 'I don't have time to discuss that right now.'

'Eve also mentioned that you've been... a bit behind when it comes to looking after yourself.'

'What the fuck is that supposed to mean?' How dare he

take this line of questioning with her? What did that have to do with anything?

'All I mean is that—'

'The autopsy report arrived,' Kathy cut him off, eyes flicking to the man who was staring right at her. 'My copy arrived today. Yours probably did, too.'

'It did.'

'And?'

Linda mouthed something in the direction of the man.

'And what? It doesn't prove anything.' But there was a glimmer of hope in his voice, only partially masked by the possibility of Mary. Of the ghost that he supposedly did not believe in.

Kathy groaned. 'It's the only thing that explains his head injury. The killer grabbed his face—they found bruises consistent with this—and then whacked his head on a rock, before throwing him into the ditch.' The man turned away and went back into the building, but left his front door open.

'The bruises are more likely to have come from a man he came across in the woods,' Alan said, his words running into each other as he sped up.

'They're the wrong size.' Kathy remembered something else she had read in the report. 'Did you even read it?'

'Of course I fucking read it,' Alan huffed. 'So, what then? It was his friend? The other boy who was with him?'

Kathy rolled her eyes at Linda. 'If that were true, it wouldn't have been ruled an accident.'

'But what if—'

'It was a woman,' Kathy interrupted. 'A woman grabbed him by the face and threw him into the ditch. At first they thought it was me, or even Eve. But we were both wearing false nails, and the marks on his cheek—' she took a deep breath, not wanting to picture her boy's face again. The face that still haunted every waking moment. 'Besides, Linda's boy had similar bruises.'

'That doesn't mean anything.'

Linda cut in. 'They found skin cells under his nails—both my son's and yours. But the DNA they found wasn't human. In fact, they weren't able to match it to the profile of any creature at all.'

Alan said nothing.

'We're meeting with a paranormal investigator,' Kathy said. 'Just like some of the other victims did in the past. But this time, we're going to fix it. We're going to stand up to Mary.' She cut off the call and opened her car door, ready to hear what the investigator had to say.

8

REVENGE

Kathy knocked on the open door, three hard raps. She stood back, not looking inside, trying to be polite.

Linda had no such qualms. 'Bertie?' She called as she stepped over the threshold. 'Sorry about that. Can we come in?'

A chuckle sounded from inside. 'Sounds like you already are.'

Kathy chanced a peek inside. It was dark, but there were some candles on a small table in the centre of the—house? Hut? Barn? She wasn't sure how to refer to this place.

The old man was sitting on a wooden chair on the far side of the table, three mugs in front of him. He was completely bald, with an earring in his left earlobe and black lines from a tattoo just visible on his shoulder, leading down underneath his shirt. He had a kind smile, aimed her way. 'Welcome to my home,' he said.

Kathy frowned, glancing around to see a pile of blankets on what looked like a bench in the corner that must serve as his bed. 'You live here?' She sputtered out.

Linda sat next to him and took a mug. 'Thanks, Bertie.' She took a sip and gestured opposite her. 'Sit,' she told Kathy.

Kathy did and took a mug, but after looking inside she set it back down. It had a mixture of dried leaves brewing inside that she really didn't like the look of. 'We need to talk to you about our sons,' Kathy said. 'We know what happened, and we need to stop it from happening again.'

'Mm?' Bertie hummed, sipping his own drink. 'And why did you choose to come to me? Why not the police?'

'It's Mary Pannell,' Linda said. 'Do you remember when I came to you before?'

Bertie shrugged. 'I'm sorry for your loss, but I'm afraid my memory fails me.'

Linda took a deep breath. 'When it was my son who died? In the Pannell wood?'

'If I couldn't help you then, I doubt I can help you now,' he sighed. 'I'm sorry not to be of further help.'

'No, please,' Linda insisted. 'It's different. When I saw Mary all those years ago, I saw her leaving Ledston Hall. I thought she was escaping, but that she fell into the ditch and died.' She groaned, running her fingers through her hair. 'I told you the wrong information. I thought her death was accidental, and that she died from the same curse that killed my boy.'

Bertie set a hand on her shoulder. 'I think I remember you,' he said in a low voice. 'I believe we did some curse-breaking work on the scene?'

'That's right,' Linda said. 'We chanted and then sprinkled something on the ground.' She stood up, pushing her chair loudly against the ground. 'I thought it worked! I thought she was gone. But when I saw Kathy's story on the news, I knew—I just knew she was back.'

'Wait, you knew?' Kathy asked. A tingle of dread lingered in the back of her mind. Alan had told her not to trust Linda. 'When I came into the library, you already knew who I was?'

Linda stepped back, leaning against the stone wall. There were no coverings on the walls, so it must have been cold. She closed her eyes and sighed. 'Just because I knew who you were, it doesn't mean I misled you.'

Kathy scoffed. 'That's exactly what that means! I shared my own personal story with you.'

'So did I!' Linda insisted. 'Look, you don't have to like me. But I did what I did because I needed to get you on side. I needed to work with you, to get you to trust me, if I wanted to find out what you saw that day.'

Kathy stood and made her way around the table to face Linda. She spoke firmly and without hesitation. 'You. Could. Have. Just. Asked. Me.'

'And you would've told me?' Linda asked. 'If I had told you that I had already spent hours trying to find out everything about you? If I admitted I wanted to know everything I could about both you and your son? If I told you the reason I was so interested was because of a curse I thought I had broken?'

Kathy sat back down and let out a deep breath. 'Fine. No. I wouldn't have taken you seriously. But I don't like liars.'

Bertie cleared his throat. 'If I may cut in, what is it you've found out since we last spoke?'

Kathy rolled her eyes. 'Well, for one thing, what happened to my son proves that you two never broke the so-called curse.'

He nodded. 'That's potentially true,' he said, stroking his chin. 'What would you suggest we do differently this time?'

With a groan of frustration, Kathy glanced at Linda. 'Go on, then. Since you're the expert in both of our cases, what should we do?'

One side of Linda's mouth curved up into a smile. 'Kathy saw Mary, burning on a pyre in the woods. She was killed, Bertie. Executed.'

He raised an eyebrow. 'Interesting,' he mused. 'You think perhaps she was executed for a crime?'

'Yes,' Linda said immediately. 'The Witham boy died the same year she did. And he was five years old. If her local community wrongly convicted her of his murder—'

'It would make sense that she would be angry at the community. That she would want to take revenge,' he said, jumping up from his chair and running his fingertips along a dusty shelf littered with small bottles. He muttered under his breath. 'Not a curse, then. A shadow of the woman. Shadows of her life.' He turned to glance from one of them to the other. 'You both saw flashes of her life?'

'Yes,' they said at the same time.

Kathy wanted to be angry at Linda. She did. But she knew she had a point. And right now, all that mattered to her was taking out her revenge on Mary. This woman should not be allowed to continue attacking young boys of Kippax. It was not right.

'Did you acknowledge her at all? Did you speak to her? Or did you try to touch her?' Bertie picked up a small bottle. 'Ah, yes,' he murmured, dropping it into his jacket pocket. He wore a tweed suit that might once have been neat. It certainly seemed to fit him well, like it had been tailored. But it was covered in small patches, and was thinning in places. Like he had been wearing it for years.

They both shook their heads.

'Are you sure?' He asked, making eye contact with Kathy. 'Your encounter was the most recent. Any acknowledgement can set them off. Even making eye contact?' He grabbed a handful of other small items from various shelves around the place and then headed straight out of the door.

Kathy's mouth dropped open in shock, and she followed him. 'Fuck. Yes. I did. But I didn't realise—fuck, this is my fault. I looked right at her.'

Bertie sighed. 'You think perhaps you did, too?' He asked Linda.

She bit her lip. 'This is not my fault. It's not my fault, and it's not Kathy's.'

'I didn't say that,' Bertie said, tapping on the car door. 'But it's important that we know exactly what happened.' He lowered his voice. 'This time, we'll get her. I swear to you—both of you—we'll get her.'

Kathy still didn't know whether this man was trustworthy, but for now, he was the best they had. She unlocked the car and got into the driver's seat.

'Drive us back to the Pannell wood,' he said. He asked for some more details and scribbled them down on a notepad. They went through the dates of deaths of all the incidents they knew about, so Kathy handed her phone to Linda. She read the notes to him exactly as they were written.

In Kathy's rearview mirror, she saw him run his eyes down his list, flicking the pages to read through all of it before he spoke.

'Bertie, we have to—' Linda started.

Kathy interrupted her. 'If you just listen—'

He held up a hand to silence them both. 'Hold on.' He was staring out the window, lost in thought, as if he were trying to figure something out.

Kathy turned onto the main road right as her phone vibrated in Linda's hand.

'It's Alan,' she told her.

Kathy groaned. 'I don't have time to deal with him right now.'

'Is that your son's father?' Bertie asked suddenly.

'Erm, yes?' Kathy said. 'Why does that matter?'

'Tell him to meet us there,' he said.

'For fuck's sake,' Kathy sighed, as she turned a corner. 'Is that really necessary?'

Bertie snapped his notebook shut and met her eye in the mirror. 'The more connections we could have to the spirit, the more likely we are to be able to successfully communicate.'

'Communicate?' Kathy sputtered. 'She put a curse on this town!'

Linda picked up the phone and Alan's voice sounded on the hands-free.

'Hello?'

'Alan,' Kathy sighed. 'Can you meet us there? In the wood. Asap.'

'You what?' Alan asked. 'You want me to go to the place where my son died? Is this something to do with this paranormal investigator?'

Bertie cleared his throat. 'Sir, if I may?'

His grunt of annoyance was audible even over the crackly line.

'Even if you don't believe in my work, do you really think my work could harm anyone? What do you have to lose?'

'Money, for a start,' Alan scoffed.

'Alan, please,' Kathy tried.

'Sir, I'm not charging anything for my services today,' Bertie said. 'In fact, I would like to refund Linda what she paid me all those years ago, because clearly, there was a mistake.'

There was a long pause, where nobody said anything. The only sound was that of Kathy's car engine humming along the road.

'Fine,' he said eventually. 'I can be there in five.'

9

CONFRONTATION

When Kathy and the others arrived at the ditch, Alan was there waiting for them. She saw him staring into the place their son had fallen, and went straight to him. She reached out her arms as if to hug him, but then pulled them back. Stupid. It was not a good idea to be acting like this with him. She stopped short of the hug and instead gave him a polite nod. 'Alan.'

'Kathy,' he nodded back, his face twisting into a smile that looked as awkward as she felt.

Bertie emptied a small bag into the ditch, small pink crystals falling onto the spot where Leo had fallen.

'What's that?' Alan asked, his voice trembling.

'Pink Halite. That is to say, coarse Himalayan pink salt,' Bertie said. 'It is often to aid in protection from evil spirits, but also for purification and cleansing.' He emptied the bag into the ditch and continued, 'One of the lesser known properties is that it can help to release emotional attachments. In this case, I'm hoping it will help the spirit of Mary Pannell to release her attachment to this place. To the residents, present and future, of this town.'

Kathy craned her neck to look into the space now littered with the large salt crystals. Part of her thought the spot would look different now, after what had happened to Leo. But it was chilling, how similar it was. The blood was gone, but she could still see it there. The blood pooling around his head. Leo lying there, unmoving, as she jumped down to perform CPR, desperate to bring him back.

She shook her head, trying to bring herself back to the present moment. 'What should we do?' She asked Bertie, her voice weak.

'Last time, we were trying to break a curse that afflicted Mary just as much as the victims. As such, our efforts weren't actually focused on Mary at all,' Bertie said clearly. 'We won't make that mistake again.' He handed each of them a large pink salt crystal and a bundle of what looked like herbs wrapped in a thin piece of paper.

Kathy frowned. 'We're supposed to hold these?'

Bertie pulled her by the wrist, leading her right to the edge of the ditch, and then directed Alan to stand on her right, and Linda on her left. He held out a lighter and lit each of their bundles in turn. 'This is sage,' he explained. 'It's associated with wisdom, and can be used for cleansing. I'd like you to focus on the scent as it fills your nostrils, and do your best to clear your mind. I want you to be open when Mary's spirit enters this space.'

Linda held the bundle to her nose. 'Mm, I think I remember this from last time.'

Alan frowned. 'If you've done all this before, I don't see what we're doing here now. It obviously didn't work, so we may as well—' He made to leave, but Kathy glared at him.

'You're not going anywhere,' she hissed. 'If this has even a chance of working—if there is any chance whatsoever that this will mean that nobody has to go through what we did, we're doing it.'

'Ugh,' Alan grunted, taking his place back next to her.

Bertie stood on the opposite side of the ditch and pulled a small book out of his pocket. It had a leather cover, faded and ripped in places, and there were many discoloured pages and additional sheets of paper stuffed in. 'What's different about today,' he said, glancing up at the darkening sky above them. It seemed darker than it actually was, given the numerous trees around them, forming almost a canopy above their heads. 'is your focus. I want your focus on Mary. Think of her.'

'We don't even know her,' Alan scoffed, as the scent of sage filled the surrounding air.

Kathy gripped more tightly onto the salt crystal and took a deep breath, inhaling the sage. 'We know some things about her,' she breathed. 'I saw her die. She was killed by her own community. Burned on a pyre for her supposed crimes. But she was innocent.'

Bertie nodded at Linda, before flicking his gaze back to the book, looking through the pages for what he needed.

'I saw her, too,' Linda said, her tone confident. Like she was ready for this. Kathy supposed she must be more than ready—she had already been through this. 'I saw the fear in her eyes as she ran from her workplace. From what was likely her home. She ran from there, sobbing, in a futile attempt to escape her fate.' She held up her hands and closed her eyes, as if that would help to summon Mary to them.

Alan scoffed. 'Fine. I didn't see her, but I know what she did. Mary hurt my son.' He paused, taking a deep breath before continuing. 'She took my son from me, and multiple others. She must have been really fucking angry. Whatever happened to her, it made her desperate for revenge.'

'Mary,' Bertie called, his voice booming throughout the small clearing. 'We await you.' He lowered his voice, speaking to the three lined up opposite him. 'Think of her. Of what you just told me. Zero in on what you think you know about her, and don't let yourself think of anything else. Call to her.'

'Please, Mary,' Kathy begged, trying her best to project her voice far and wide.

'Come to us,' Linda called next.

Alan made a face as he tilted his face up and shouted, 'you've taken your revenge. Face us.'

'Shh,' Bertie hushed them, his head whipping around to catch sight of something.

A familiar whistling sound came upon the place where they were gathered.

Kathy's whole body twitched when a chill wind whooshed past her right ear. 'Fuck,' she muttered.

'Is that—' Alan started.

Bertie licked his index finger and held it up high. 'Shh, all of you.'

Another gust of wind came over them, but he shook his head.

'There's no wind. It's her,' he whispered, his eyes wide.

They didn't speak again, but it was anything but silent. A cacophony of sounds overtook them. There was the whistling, louder this time. A whoosh of the wind that wasn't actually wind. A high-pitched scream that Kathy hadn't heard before. And then, alongside a wave of heat, there was that crackling sound of flames, as if Mary's body were right in front of them, burning even all these years later.

'Mary!' Bertie called, holding one finger on his page as he read from it. 'Vocamus te,' he read. 'Impleat fossam spiritus tuus.'

Kathy stared back at him. She never learned Latin, so wasn't sure what he was saying, but whatever it was seemed to be strengthening the fog that had started to surround them.

Alan shuffled closer to her, their elbows knocking against each other, though he didn't say anything. His eyes were on Bertie.

Bertie's eyes dropped to the ditch. 'Iubeo ut nunc huc venisti,' he shouted, even more loudly than before.

Kathy shook and for one terrifying moment, thought that she was going to fall into the ditch in front of them.

Alan grabbed onto her, as did Linda, like they had felt the same force pushing them forward.

She stared ahead at the figure that was down there now.

Mary.

There was that same white dress that she had seen that day. The corner of which had seen poking down as the flames had eaten it up.

Bertie locked eyes with her and the leaves surrounding his feet floated up, circling him quickly, like some kind of tornado about to sweep him away.

Kathy's hair blew wildly in front of her face, but she had her hands full, so she couldn't tuck it back. She tightened her grip on the crystal and the sage bundle, as if that would help anything at all.

'De his qui hic tuleris ultionem,' he called, gesturing to the three of them.

Mary's head snapped around to face them.

Kathy gasped as she saw her face again, and that day when she had lost her son—Leo—came flooding back to her. Tears welled up in her eyes as she locked her gaze with Mary. There was a ghostly pallor on her face, slightly translucent, as if she had been projected, like she was a trick of light. But they were in the middle of nowhere. She was real. Her eyes were dark, angry. 'Please,' she begged her. 'You —you've taken everything from me.'

Alan nodded. 'You've had your revenge.'

'I'm sorry,' Linda said, her voice hitching. The wind still blew around them and her voice was quieter than the rest, barely audible.

Mary seemed to understand her anyway, as her gaze softened, just slightly.

'All these years, I've thought you were the victim.' Tears flooded down her cheeks. She was sobbing in the face of the ghost. In front of Mary Pannell. 'But I find out that it was you? All this time, it's you who have been taking our sons from us. From this town.'

Mary's eyebrows furrowed and she let out an ear-piercing scream, throwing her hands up into the air as she did.

'No!' Bertie shouted. 'Tell her, Linda,' he said. 'Tell her what you think of her now.'

Linda threw her crystal and sage into the ditch.

Kathy flinched, terrified this was all about to end—that she had fucked it all up. But Mary stayed. She floated over the ditch, over the space where she had ended so many lives in her rage.

'But then I realised you *are* the victim,' Linda shouted. 'They killed you, didn't they? They blamed you for killing that boy, but you were innocent. I saw it in your eyes that day,' she insisted. 'It's one of the reasons I was so damn sure that all this was because of a fucking curse.' She jumped down into the ditch in frustration.

The spirit in front of them backed away—barely at all—but Kathy saw it. Linda was getting through to her.

'You were innocent,' Linda repeated. 'But still, they burned you. They hated you for something you never did. Condemned you to this—to this existence, whatever this is.'

Tears started to drip down Mary's cheeks, but she didn't talk back.

'Oramus ut relinquamus,' Bertie announced. 'You've been stuck here, fuelled by hatred. Taking out your rage on those just as innocent as the little boy you were convicted of killing.'

Mary floated right up to look into Bertie's eyes. The leaves circling him fell to the ground. She looked right at him, the whistling sound still surrounding them.

Kathy was reminded of what he had said about eye contact. What if this was what Mary wanted? What if she was about to kill him? What if she wanted to kill all of them? Was this all a big mistake?

But that ear-piercing scream sounded again, and this time, Kathy dropped the crystal and the sage, in favour of bringing her hands to her ears.

Mary was screaming louder now, and she floated back into that ditch, not even looking at Linda. Instead, she focused on the ground.

Mary kept screaming and staring at that spot for a long time, until finally, she went silent, still staring at the spot where Leo had fallen.

None of them dared say anything—they just watched.

In that spot, right where Mary was looking, there appeared the translucent figure of a young boy. He had the same dreamlike quality as Mary. Another spirit. He wore a hat, and his trousers were held up by braces over a baggy long-sleeved white shirt. There was blood leaving a wound on his head. Despite that, he opened his eyes.

'What the fuck?' Alan whispered.

'Shh,' Bertie said.

Linda nodded. 'Look, she's taking them with her.'

Mary held out her hand, and the boy stood to take it.

Next, in the same exact spot, another spirit of a boy appeared. He also wore a flat cap, but his clothes were dark, dirty. Covered in what looked like coal. He, too, opened his eyes and took Mary's hand.

A wave of realisation hit Kathy. 'She never wanted to hurt them. She wanted to save them.' Her voice cracked. 'She didn't trust anyone in the town to look after their sons, so she took them with her. To keep them safe.' A sob left her lips as she thought of Leo. Of course she would have kept him safe. Mary had taken him from her, all based on this—this lie. This untruth. 'He was mine,' she whimpered.

But Mary didn't even turn to look at her.

'Is this it?' Alan whispered. 'Is she leaving for good?'

'I think she's finally allowing herself to get what she always wanted,' Bertie murmured. 'She's been waiting to take the boys away. Waiting to gather as many of them as she could. And now that she's done that, she's finally leaving.'

One by one, the figures of boys appeared and got up, each holding the hand of one of the other boys. As dozens of boys got up from their spots on the ground, their outfits appeared to be becoming more modern. Like they were boys that had died more recently.

Linda dropped to her knees and let out a shriek when one boy appeared, wearing white shorts and a patterned t-shirt. She reached out to grab him, but her hands went right through the ghostly figure.

He simply smiled and held the hand of one of the other boys. They now made a chain, Mary standing in the centre, and the boys' hands forming a long link of hands, up each side of the ditch and along the space of the clearing.

Then it was Leo's turn.

Leo's small body appeared in the same spot Kathy knew he would. In the same spot every single one of the boys appeared in. He had the same head wound the other boys had. The same one that had made Kathy's heart absolutely drop when she had jumped down to help him that day.

Despite what she had seen Linda do, Kathy jumped down and wrapped her arms around her boy, sobbing—but her arms went right through him. Like he wasn't even there.

But he was there.

His smile was so fucking familiar that she knew it was her boy. This was Leo.

Alan's arms were around her shoulders in a second and together, they watched as Leo smiled at Mary and then, when she gestured to the edge of the ditch, he crawled out. As if he had no head injury at all. As if he had been breathing, playing some sort of sick game this whole time.

Leo held onto Linda's son's hand.

Mary glanced at Linda, then Kathy and Alan, all gathered closely around each other in the ditch and narrowed her eyes.

Bertie bellowed, one final shout to end them all, 'discede!'

At that, the leaves around them flew up in the air, and Mary floated up first, the boys floating up after her. It was as if the leaves carried her, and she carried the boys by the hand, each one holding up the boy next to him.

The whistling sound followed them up to the dark sky, fading from the space just as the boys did. Just as Mary did.

THANK YOU FOR READING!

If you or someone you know have seen her ghost, or if you've heard any more versions of the legend of Mary Pannell, get in touch! I would love to write more of these short stories.

I love hearing what readers have to say about my books so I would be grateful if you would leave me a review.

As an indie author, reviews are really helpful for me. Thank you so much for all your support!

For more about the English Witch Trials, you can read the articles on my website:

melissamanners.com

Read my debut novel, **The Pannell Witch,** *and* the prequel, **Becoming The Pannell Witch**, available now.

To be the first to hear about my next book, **The Witham Witch**, sign up to my mailing list on my website.

I really love to hear from my readers, so follow me:

facebook.com/melissamannerswrites

instagram.com/melissamannerswrites

amazon.com/author/melissamanners

goodreads.com/melissamanners

ABOUT THE AUTHOR

Melissa was born and raised in London where her book obsession began. She would take a book everywhere she went (she still does this, and probably always will). Her writing career started at the tender age of eight when she wrote her first 'book': a folded booklet summarising the story of Persephone.

Her love of Greek mythology continued into adulthood, as did her love of storytelling. She spent her teen years writing angst-ridden fanfic until she found NaNoWriMo, which she entered year after year.

It was not until she was in her twenties that she found her love of historical fiction. The historical period that most stuck out was that of the English Witch Trials—horrifying, yet fascinating. The treatment of women in particular (but also a range of other people seen as 'different'), is what Melissa wanted to address in her own writing.

She loves to reframe the narrative that has been passed down to us, mostly by men, and allow stories to be told from a new perspective. It's a shame we don't have many records from this period, but through historical fiction we can give those neglected members of society a voice.

THE PANNELL WITCH
CHAPTER ONE

Kippax, West Yorkshire, 1593

Elizabeth knew Mary was hiding something. From the smile plastered over worried eyes to her bitten lip and fidgeting hands; she was terrified. But Elizabeth wouldn't force the truth out of her.

'We can slow down if you like. It's no rush,' Elizabeth said. She needed to help Mary calm down.

'No.' Mary's breaths were quick. Shallow. 'I'm fine.'

She sighed. 'If you say so. Follow me.' With every step she had to lift her foot up high, over the mass of leaves covering the ground. 'Why here?'

'What do you mean?' Mary asked.

'When you left Ledston Hall, why did you come here, to the woods? Why didn't you go home?'

Mary cleared her throat. She was struggling to keep up. 'Something happened. And I couldn't face Mother Pannell.'

'Why not? My mother would want to help—you're family.' It wasn't strictly true; she had married into the Pannell family, whereas Elizabeth was born a Pannell. Elizabeth untucked her hair from the back of her collar. It was itchy in this heat, and she didn't need to be Eli right now.

'It's complicated,' Mary muttered.

Underneath the thin layer of dried leaves, the ground was wet and muddy. With every step Elizabeth had to unstick one foot from the ground and let it fall in front of her with a squelch. There were lots of tree roots to step around and Elizabeth was worried Mary would trip. She kept looking back to check on her. 'Do you need me to slow down?' She called.

Mary didn't respond.

It was a sunny day and climbing over the uneven ground as fast as they were only made them more exhausted. Mary was walking slowly, placing her feet into the spots where Elizabeth had stepped. Elizabeth was glad—she didn't want her to trip.

'What happened at Ledston Hall? What's got you so shaken up?' Elizabeth asked.

Mary was dripping with sweat, her face red and blotchy. She had been crying. What had happened back at the house?

'Please, talk to me?' Elizabeth tried again.

Mary forced a smile. 'I'm fine.' She carried on walking.

Something was worrying her. Mary closed her eyes and inhaled. Elizabeth copied her, taking in the comforting earthy smell of the forest and listening to the birdsong.

Elizabeth stopped at a small clearing, shielded from the sun by a circle of tall trees. It was perfect for sitting in because of all the large tree roots sticking out of the ground. They hadn't been to this place for years, but Elizabeth would never forget it.

Mary leaned forward and put her hands on her knees,

panting. 'I always liked it here.' She wiped the sweat from her forehead and pulled off her cap. 'It's private.' The only people that lived nearby were themselves and Mother Pannell, in their huts at the edge of the woods.

'Mother used to take me swimming here.' Elizabeth said. She took Mary's hand and led her to a flat area on the edge of the lake. 'Do you remember coming here with me?'

Mary took a second to catch her breath. 'Of course. This is where we used to...' Her cheeks reddened with embarrassment and she looked at the ground. Elizabeth reached over and tucked a stray hair behind Mary's ear.

'Sit here. Let's try to unwind, forget about everything.' Elizabeth lowered herself down, one hand on her back, rolled up her trousers and took off her shoes. Then she dangled her feet in the water. She flexed her feet, one at a time, making small splashes.

'Isn't it cold?' Mary asked.

'See for yourself.' Elizabeth patted the ground next to her and gestured for her to sit.

Mary squealed as her feet touched the surface but lowered them in anyway. 'Ah, that does help. My feet are so sore from the walk here.' Mary did a lot of walking most days, and she was not a young woman. She sighed and lay her head on Elizabeth's chest.

Elizabeth smiled and kissed her on top of her head, which was at the perfect angle. She untied Mary's long black hair and let it fall down past her shoulders. Finally, Mary had taken a moment to relax.

'Anyway, it's time for a swim!' Elizabeth stood and began to undress.

'No! It's too cold!' Mary said.

'You're still sweating from the walk! Come, join me.' Elizabeth threw her work trousers over a nearby tree branch and unfastened her linen shirt.

Mary's breathing quickened. 'You make me feel like a child sometimes!'

Elizabeth smirked. She ran her fingers through her hair and shook her head from side to side. Mary was watching her, but avoided looking directly at her.

Mary grinned and placed her woollen skirt over the same branch.

'Come on, then!' Elizabeth called.

Mary's eyes widened as she surveyed Elizabeth's long, bare legs. The dark, dense hairs on her lower legs grew more sparse at her knees and became fairer on her thighs. Mary took a deep breath and unfastened her bodice.

'Ready?' Elizabeth ran towards the lake and dived in. The cold shocked her system all at once and she was glad she hadn't lowered herself in gradually. She disappeared under the surface, the water closing over her head, before emerging with a cry.

'The water is cold, isn't it?' Mary had undressed, but now stood with her arms wrapped nervously around herself, pacing.

'No,' Elizabeth lied, and she swam to the far side of the lake.

'I think I'll lower myself in.' She sat on the edge of the lake and dangled her feet in the water.

Elizabeth held her breath and swam underwater towards Mary. She brushed Mary's toes with her hand as she swam to the water's edge, then threw her head above the surface.

Mary gasped.

She always pretended not to be ticklish, but Elizabeth knew better.

Elizabeth jumped out of the water and wrapped her arms around Mary. 'Surprise!'

Mary giggled. 'Elizabeth, it's cold. Let's dry off while the sun is still out.' Mary's expression darkened once more. What was she hiding?

She distracted Elizabeth with a kiss on the cheek. 'Come here.' She patted the ground next to her, then spread her linen underskirt over them both, shielding them from the wind. They stretched out to dry on the grassy bank of the lake.

Elizabeth shivered. Goosebumps had formed on her legs. The grass was hot from the sun, and it warmed her aching back.

'I like it here.' Mary said.

'Me too.' Elizabeth stroked Mary's dark, wet hair, streaked with silver. 'I wish we didn't have to go back to Ledston Hall.'

Mary stiffened next to her. 'But you like working there, especially as Eli.'

She twirled a strand of Mary's hair around her finger. 'Just because they don't make me cook and clean, doesn't mean I'm not still a servant.'

'What else would you want to be?' Mary asked.

Elizabeth didn't have an answer. 'Forget it. Let's just lie here for a while.' She closed her eyes.

The trickles of water running over the rocks and crashing into the banks grounded her in that moment. Mary settled once again onto her side, her head leaning on Elizabeth's chest. It was much warmer with Mary this close. Before long they both fell asleep.

THE CRACK of a branch sounded from behind them.

Elizabeth's eyes snapped open. She shivered—the sun was no longer overhead. A darkness enveloped them in their small clearing. Mary was already awake—she pushed Mary off her and sat up straight. Her mind was racing as she ran through the possibilities in her mind. It was probably nothing, a rabbit that had been scared off at the sight of them both.

More branches cracked—they were closer this time. This was no rabbit.

A horse whinnied in the distance. Who could it be? The villagers would not normally travel this far. Maybe it was a wild horse, or even a group of wild horses?

A louder crack sounded from right behind them. It had to be heading towards them, whatever it was.

'Quick, get dressed.' Elizabeth whispered to Mary. 'Do not make a sound.'

Mary did as she was told. While she dressed, Elizabeth kept a lookout. She was trying to catch sight of whatever or whoever was nearby, but in such deep woodland it was impossible to see very far around them.

'Hurry,' Elizabeth urged Mary. Elizabeth too reached into the pile of her clothes, not taking her eyes off the trees where the sounds of cracking branches had come from.

Both women were standing partially clothed when the man appeared. Mary wore a linen slip, and Elizabeth had on a shirt.

'Ahem.' He cleared his throat.

Mary squealed and grabbed her skirt to cover her body. The man was younger than Mary and Elizabeth, probably in his thirties. The sound of footsteps made Mary look around, to see ten men waiting and watching them.

Elizabeth addressed Mary. 'Don't worry. We'll sort this out. Get dressed.' Mary's eyes widened.

'My name—' the man began.

'Excuse me,' Elizabeth interrupted and spoke loudly and clearly. 'We were just bathing in the lake. Please allow us a minute of privacy to dress.'

He coughed and sputtered over his words, not used to this sort of directness coming from a woman. 'Ah, yes. Yes, I suppose.' He gestured to the other men, who turned away. Mary pulled on her bodice and her heavy woollen skirt. Elizabeth brushed off the dried mud from her feet. Specks of mud were stuck in the hairs on her legs, so she rubbed off what she could. She thrust her legs into her trousers and they both put their shoes on.

'Who are these men?' Mary muttered, breathing fast. 'Why are they here?'

'Don't worry. Whatever happens, we can sort it.'

'Elizabeth, I think this is about me.' Mary's cheeks reddened, more in anger than in embarrassment. 'But you have to trust me. I have done nothing wrong.'

Mary had pulled on her cloak just as they turned back around.

'Ahem.' The man who had spoken before looked disapprovingly at Mary. 'My name is Sir Henry Griffith of Burton Agnes, Justice of the Peace and High Sherriff.' He wore a bright red, tightly fitted jacket. It matched his trousers, which were tucked into white socks. His clothes set him apart from the plain-clothed group gathered behind him.

Tears welled up in Mary's eyes—she was scared. Elizabeth shook her head at her. Mary held her breath to calm down.

'I seek to arrest Mary Pannell, née Tailor, on suspicion of witchcraft.'

Mary's eyes widened and she let out an involuntary gasp.

Elizabeth stepped in front of Mary. 'Stay behind me,' she said under her breath.

Sir Henry took a roll of parchment from his inside jacket pocket. He frowned as he read from it.

'The charge is that you did place a charm on Sir William Witham, of Ledston Hall, taking him to your bed, and that you did bewitch him to death.'

Mary stifled a sob.

'No.' Elizabeth shook her head. 'No!' Why was he saying these things? 'You've got it wrong; Mary wouldn't do this.'

'I hereby place you under arrest. You shall be imprisoned and interrogated for up to three days, during which time we shall seek a confession and thereafter bring you to trial.'

Elizabeth turned around but Mary avoided eye contact. She couldn't hold on any longer. She sobbed, tears streaming down her face. Elizabeth squeezed her hand. 'Mary, tell them.' She gritted her teeth, trying to stay calm. 'Tell them they've got the wrong person. I know you didn't do this.'

'I'm sorry.' She dug her fingernails into Elizabeth's palms. 'I didn't think they'd find us here.' Her sobs punctuated her words. 'I'm innocent. I promise.'

Sir Henry nodded to two of his men, who approached Mary and grabbed her by the shoulders. They pulled her from Elizabeth's side.

'Stop!' Elizabeth shouted. She elbowed the man next to her in the chest and he doubled over. 'Let go of her.'

A man grabbed Elizabeth from behind and threw her to the ground.

Mary screamed. 'Leave her alone, she has nothing to do with this!'

'Mary? Mary!' Elizabeth tried to stand up, but the man kept his foot firmly on her back, burying her face in the mud, and she couldn't move. She couldn't even see her as they dragged her away.

~

To keep reading, get your copy of
The Pannell Witch here!